FUNNY
ACCENT

PICADOR USA

NEW YORK

FUNNY ACCENT

A NOVEL BY

BARBARA

SHULGASSER-

PARKER

www.picadorusa.com

Picador® is a U.S. registered trademark and is used by
St. Martin's Press under license from Pan Books Limited.

ISBN 0-312-27517-X

First Edition: June 2001

10 9 8 7 6 5 4 3 2 1

For my mother,

my brother,

and my father,

and

for Norman,

with deepest love

ACKNOWLEDGMENTS

I am extremely grateful to various people without whom the publication of this book would not have been possible. For their patience, editing and long-term cheerleading, I thank my husband, Norman Parker, Tom Congdon and Barbara Berkowitz.

Special thanks for their endless encouragement to Steven Barclay, Dianne Dickert, Mimi Mendelson, Melissa Prince Quisenberry and Harriet Schiffer Scott.

For their faith, judgment and singular efforts on the book's behalf, I owe a debt to my agent, Molly Friedrich, her associate, Paul Cirone, my editor, Alicia Brooks, and my publisher, Frances Coady.

And I am especially grateful to my mother, Luba Shulgasser, and my brother, Mark Shulgasser, for their love and support.

For my husband, Norman, dere are no woids.

This story takes place

in the nineteen eighties

THE

GEESE

ONE

The animal behaviorist Konrad Lorenz performed an experiment in the nineteen thirties to help him document his observations on imprinting. Little geese seemed to know the minute they hatched from the egg that they were supposed to follow around their mothers, a sort of genetic safety feature. But would a gosling follow only its mother? Or would it simply follow the first thing it saw?

So Lorenz placed himself before an imminently hatching egg. The egg cracked open, the gooey gosling peeked through the jagged shell, took one look at Lorenz, squeaked "Mom," and dutifully followed the man everywhere. This kind of built-in programming has its assets, but when the programming goes awry—when it's clear that a gosling doesn't *identify* its mother but rather hopefully assumes the first face it sees will be a friendly guide to a good life—hazards abound.

Farther up along the evolutionary chain the results can be just as disastrous. The first time Misha kissed me he was fifty-one. I was thirteen. Some people might think of this as sexual abuse. *I* think of it as sexual abuse. Well, I do *now,* these many years later. But for a long time it didn't seem like abuse; it couldn't have been because I liked it so much. To make a long story short, I've been following around the wrong geese ever since.

So, I started the short story, set in 1967: "She was thirteen the first time. He was fifty-one. They were in the kitchen leaning against a Formica counter and laughing," and one of the magazines I sent it to was good enough to publish it.

It had taken awhile to get it right. More was required than a simple retelling of the events. It seemed important to explain that the "he" was a survivor, someone who had triumphed over Adolph Hitler's plans to kill him. It seemed important to place him among my parents' friends, as another one of the lucky ones who lived. Of the thirty-seven thousand Jewish inhabitants of the Kovno ghetto, he and my parents were among the three thousand to make it through the war. Their interrupted lives continued in America. The doctors washed dishes. The lawyers delivered seltzer. The accountants taught Hebrew school. All of them studied English, worked nights, earned baccalaureates anew, ate distressing foods, counted unfamiliar money and, in response to their ordeal, survived yet again; it had become habit. When the exams were over and they were opening practices and starting businesses, the postwar boom tossed them spinning into the unexpected good life. They found themselves homeowners, parents and citizens who, benevolent and patriotic, would cheerfully come to regard newer immigrants as "foreigners." They were solid, participatory members of the community, licensed, board-certified, registered, and so they treated illnesses, sold property, built shopping centers and negotiated their way through life with funny accents and unbending wills. He was just like the others.

Suddenly I was leaning on a kitchen counter and he, with a martini in one hand, was leaning toward me, looking into my eyes, looking at my mouth, raising his free hand to my waist as if he meant to touch it, but withdrawing it before he did. As he studied my face with what seemed a clinical attentiveness, I wondered, Was there something wrong with me—an erupting blemish of ghastly fascination? His face was as close to mine as a dentist about to drill. I could feel his breath, a communicative moistness, sending a message I was eager to absorb. I was breathing, barely, but I didn't move. I was equally afraid and exhilarated. My parents had known him for thirty years and I trusted he would behave sensibly. So when he kissed me and eased his way through my startled mouth, when I felt him surrounding me with his arms and pressing my thin torso to his hot chest, and when I considered wriggling free but didn't, the sensation was, at first, more of betrayed confidence than revulsion. I was, in fact, too young, too raw to respond, a late developer. My body hadn't yet been wired for comprehending, let alone experiencing, the sensual pleasures he proffered. I sat motionless, assessing the way his tongue felt in my mouth. But mostly I welcomed his boldness because it initiated me into a hitherto forbidden world. He was treating me like an adult, I thought, a term I wanted applied to me. And if that meant enduring his heated embrace, it seemed a small price to pay for accreditation.

I was, as I said, a slow developer with a face that expressed an exoticism beyond my years, and I found I had the more than passing attention of many of my parents' male friends. But I wasn't yet quite sure why it was that men chased women in the first place and what they planned to do with them once they caught them. So the reason that this thirteen-year-old did not push away the man with his tongue in her mouth could be a little difficult to explain.

"Am I your type?" he asked me between kisses. "What do you look for in a boyfriend? You *do* have a boyfriend, don't you?"

"No," I said shaking my head shyly. I wanted him to know that I was free. Free to be his.

"Impossible," he said. Or, to give you a better idea, "Eempuhsabool." Most of my parents' friends came from Lithuania, as Misha did, but the Poles, the Ukrainians, the Czechs and the Hungarians spoke with the same Yiddish lilt. For many, Yiddish was their first language and it left their mouths forever twisted and vocal chords trained. I learned that a Yiddish accent had less to do with the precise production of consonants or vowels than with the whiney interrogative in which they were sung.

"Impossible," he said again. He looked at me, his eyes sweeping over my face and then my body so that I felt embarrassed by the scrutiny. "What you need," and here he paused, pleased that he was not only going to tell me what I needed but also suggest where I could get it, "is a guy. That would solve your problems." I was interested because I could see that he was referring to himself. He wanted to solve my problems. Subtly, tacitly, he was moving in on me, into my brain as intently as toward my body. He was approaching as if he knew more than I did, which he certainly did. But the allure of it was that there was something in his strategy that assumed some knowledge on my part as well. I sensed the presumption and relished it. My ear for the dog whistles of social intercourse was somewhat more well developed than my glandular system. I hadn't yet felt the flush of lust, that squeeze of pumping fluids feeding the sexual apparatus. But even if I didn't know what it felt like to succumb to an overheating pelvis, I did understand what it was to be manipulated, and it pleased me that he held me in high-enough regard to bother. He was going to trouble over me and I was flattered.

So, wondering where my parents were, I put my arms around his neck and opened my mouth to him.

The years passed. I'd see him at parties. He drank with the men. He danced with all the women, although everyone agreed that he and my mother made an especially graceful couple. Each time I would see him, his appearances weeks and sometimes months apart, the courtship would seem to begin again, puz-zlingly, as if from the start. His indirectness left me bewildered. I wasn't sure if he was trying to fool my parents or me. I would mis-take his hesitation for courtliness, and wonder, Has he forgotten that he kissed me the last time? Was my memory faulty or hadn't he wrapped himself around me then? Without his acknowledg-ment to assure me otherwise, I wondered, Had anything actually happened, or had I imagined it all? Detecting my confusion, he would proceed at each meeting, but slowly, delicately resuming his artful scam like a swindler returning to an old mark. And like the best con men, he made being taken seem a pleasure.

Between visits I would pout in front of the mirror, examining myself critically for what drew him to me. At that time, I could find no clues in my surprised eyes and curling mouth. "You're a beauty," my mother would tell me, but I thought I knew better and had only pity for the poor woman. She longed to have a daughter as beautiful as she once had been. I cringed at the sight of my lollipop head, stubbornly upright on a stem of ligaments and bone that, with the green veins visible, reminded me, in translucency and explicitness, of a dissection chart. My face, to me, looked dull, boringly near symmetrical, with a mop of black, lank fibers framing an oval of squint-inducing whiteness bisected by a left-leaning nose. Where was the beauty?

EACH VISIT MARKED a sexual encounter—a kiss, a feel, a quick unzipping in a bathroom or in my bedroom, the promise always looming of more to come one day when he, the initiator of these games, deemed the timing right. Given his seniority in this matter, I naively attributed logic, forethought and deliberateness to his actions. I was sure he must have had a plan. And with my hormones finally dispensing in high dosage, I wanted more, much more. But he remained eerily restrained, a biological anomaly. How could he hold back, I wondered? He went so far and no farther, always stopping us before genital could conjoin with genital. It was as if *he* was the underage virgin, saving himself for true love.

The substitutes for intercourse were comical. He would fondle me behind a garden of potted plants in a hidden hallway near the den. I'd laugh as he kissed me, grateful that my mother had painstakingly nurtured the shefflera to such camouflaging height and lushness. There were other clandestine locations.

"Here, come here with me," he'd hiss, ushering me into an upstairs bathroom. "God, you feel wonderful," he said holding me against him. Or, what he actually said was, "Gutchew feel wahnderfool." Unlike many of his compatriots, he had mastered the English pronunciation of the letter W and only rarely, in moments of duress, uttered the V sound instead.

"Gutchew feel wahnderfool," he said, and I would have made love to him on the spot but he pulled away. My sweater was up, my bra undone. And suddenly he was hooking me up again and tucking the sweater back in. "We'd better get back. They'll wonder where we are." He examined himself in the mirror for signs of wear, smoothed his hair and adjusted his tie. "I'll go first. We shouldn't leave at the same time."

I could see my flushed reflection looking back at myself chidingly. *What am I doing?* I asked myself. *What am I doing kissing an old man?*

I was learning the ropes. I was learning the fundamental lessons a woman learns. I didn't know it at the time. I thought I was unique. I saw my experience as unusual, a dark, tainting secret I would tell no one until years later. I was learning what every woman eventually learns. There are men out there, narcissistic, preening, predatory men who haven't a generous impulse or an unselfish sentiment anywhere within, who also happen to be handsome, charming, fun to be with and sexually attractive. And in the early stages of a woman's education, it is extremely difficult to figure out that these men are to be avoided. My highly unscientific observations have led me to conclude that it *is* possible to avoid such men but generally luck plays a large role in the avoidance. And the odds are against a girl being that lucky.

Avoiding them is just not that easy. When Misha entered a room, usually fashionably late to ensure maximum attention, the effect was galvanizing to a certain kind of female. His special effects included a perpetual suntan (quick trips to Florida through the winter kept his coloring high), a fastidiously maintained, sylphlike waistline and thick, shining black hair, short on the sides but long enough on top for a few oh-so-casual curls to beckon in the breeze. He wore handmade shoes with soles so thin they seemed designed for floating rather than walking. His suits were made of fabrics so supple that to brush accidentally against the sleeve of his coat was to begin the sensual experience.

Had I been able to write off our passionate moments as youthful indiscretions and move on profitably, I would be a well woman today. I might even have broken away from him and become attracted to more suitable companions, but soon Misha embodied more than just a ticket out of awkward adolescence. He had awakened me, and once this happened I was more or less immobilized by lust. He knew it, and would call long distance only as often as necessary to fan in me an obsession that might otherwise have died.

"I've been thinking about your neck all day today," he once called to tell me, and as a flush spread over me, I hugged my hands between my legs.

I tried to pretend insouciance when he called, trilling my replies languorously the way I thought a woman with innumerable lovers calling to worship her scorching anatomy would do. I wanted to hide from him that he was the only one, that my desire was irretrievable, that I was lost.

"When are you coming to see me?" he would moan. Where, I wondered when I heard the burr on his voice, were *his* hands?

I yearned to know him well, the way one knows an old friend, the way my parents knew him. They spoke wistfully of the war, of deprivation, of bailing each other out of tight spots, of laughing and drinking when the proposition of tomorrow seemed doubtful. But I knew that his excitement with me was rooted in how little we knew each other. It was guaranteed and sustained by the long separations. I must have seemed new to him at every meeting. A few months would have passed. I would be taller, emotionally more mature, better read, more cynical, altered in comportment and conformation. Add to that a bit of sexual frisson, and how enthralling it all must have been for him. I was a new person each time he saw me. As the already formed adult, he remained the same, time after time, yet I found him elusive. When I tried to picture him muddling through his daily schedule, I had no starting point, no image of him fixing breakfast or sitting behind an office desk. I could not call up any credible visual of him as a creature subject to the banalities of daily life. He seemed detached, above the drudgery of commuting, grocery shopping, shoe repair.

I longed for the intermittent meetings, hoping to see him when his American wife, a woman named Angela (whom he referred to as Angel for reasons, friends presumed, having to do with her godlike patience), was off spending her inheritance, globetrotting somewhere without him. He began to interrupt my peace, to become the focus of my life. When we did steal moments alone together, the sexual frustration was corrosive. Inexperienced as I was, I couldn't understand why he would kiss me, remove most of my clothes, put his hands all over my body, put my hands all over his, yet never actually, completely, out-and-out fuck me. I was in hormonal agony, literally aching for him to be inside me. I thought that this man of the world was engaging in some practice well known to the initiated, some kundalini self-denial that gave him unsurpassed pleasure, and that for me to question it would only underscore my sexual ignorance.

Not only did our relationship foster miserable deprivation and sexual frustration, but the infrequent, hasty and unsatisfying encounters infringed on my ability to be interested in other men. Other men, particularly men my age, were wan substitutes. I was paralyzed.

I went to college, where I lost my virginity passionlessly—it was time, I thought—to a college soccer player, but mostly I was alone with my thoughts of Misha.

When I was twenty-three, I took a job in a new city. His occasional calls continued. But enough was enough. Here at last was the chance to shake myself of the infatuation. I knew I had to do something. I would either force consummation or accept rejection. He would sleep with me or he would leave me alone.

When I first considered taking the trip to Boston—a spur-of-the-moment inspiration arrived at one night after Misha had called to perform his ritual telephonic foreplay—I immediately dismissed the venture as absurd. The patent aggression of the act repelled me. I imagined his face on seeing me, the shock registering and my embarrassment. I thought that if humiliation was required to expunge my demons, I'd rather live with them. But that wasn't true. I've never been able to tolerate inertia. Whenever I've been troubled I've always felt I had to *do* something to set it right. If he said no to me, that would be an end to the uncertainty. Under these conditions, there would be certainty in going to bed together and there would be certainty in not going to bed together. *Certainty* was the thing, I tried to tell myself.

Of course that wasn't exactly so. Going to bed together was the thing.

So where did I find the gall? I needed only to recall his kisses, to remember his ardor. "I can hardly stand to be in a room with you and other people," he had told me as we pressed pelvises on the dance floor at a party years before. "I want to throw rocks at them."

And I remember a ride we took when I was eighteen. We were coming back with my parents from a dinner party in a remote corner of New Jersey. They were in front, we were in the rear. The ride was long and in the dark backseat of the rumbling sedan, with my mother and father blithely sitting just a yard or so ahead of us, he undid every button, snap and fastener on everything I was wearing, including the zippers on my boots, to achieve better access. I thought with horror, I'm going to get out of the car and all my clothes will fall off.

To muffle the sounds of rustling fabric, as he moved his hands up under my shirt, he asked loudly, "What's on the radio?" Obligingly my mother switched it on, and music to breathe heavily by filled the car. I wanted to admire Misha's resourcefulness, but I was sickened and shamed by it. I felt certain he had pulled this clever little ruse before, with other women. Many times. And surely my parents were on to that old radio trick. Were they in on this too? Was I being conspired against? Were they all laughing at me?

In fact, his desire was sometimes so embarrassingly blatant that I was sure my parents, somehow believing the infatuation safe, conferred unspoken approval. Did they hope this fever would spring their daughter from her solitude and into the social mainstream? Would this get her a boyfriend? Did they think Misha would do me good?

When I was nineteen and away at college, I had tried to break away from him. In a brief moment of clearheadedness and optimism, I believed that I might be able to stand back and assess the damages coolly. I forced myself, the next time we met, to see a man vain, petty, and fretful. When he caressed me—that particular time it was in my room on the tiny bed with the red pillows and the stuffed-animal arrangement, while everyone else was downstairs having marble cake and tea—I thought he was not so much drawing me to him as wielding me like a shield against the day when his potency would fail. I vowed to myself that I would never see him again.

For months I avoided places I knew he would be, but one night he showed up unexpectedly when I was visiting my parents. "Where have you *been*?" he said urgently, pressing his hand against my thigh under the dining table. I wasn't sure if I wanted to tear his clothes off or his head. I knew then that swearing oaths to stay away would do no good. I had to solve the problem some other way.

So, finally, at twenty-three, I bought an airline ticket to Boston and without warning descended on him. "He will laugh at you," I told myself as the airplane touched the ground. "He will send you away. He will tell you that you are presumptuous, childish, unattractive." But I argued down my better judgment with hope. He had been grabbing me at every opportunity for the last ten years. Perhaps he had never made love to me in order to persuade himself that nothing was happening between us. But now, today, to send me away, to tell me it all meant nothing, he would have to lie.

I dialed his number from the airport several times, my fingers missing the keys and my legs giving way. I leaned against the wall of the telephone booth to steady myself. I felt the push of blood washing through my vessels. Somehow, when my head cleared, I could hear Misha sputtering at the other end of the line.

"You're *where*? What are you doing here? This is not a game."

"But you invited me," I said.

"When did I invite you?"

"You're always inviting me. 'If only you could come to Boston . . .' You said it last time I saw you in Scarsdale."

"I was drunk."

"For the last ten years?"

"Well, no. But this is not the point. You couldn't have arrived at a more inconvenient time," he said. The trade show was in town, the one week of the year he actually had to work. Nevertheless he found the time to pick me up at the airport. When I saw him I knew from the hysteria glazing his features that I had my answer. I stepped into the car and he said, "I can't do this." He straightened his tie. Then he did it again. He dabbed with a handkerchief at his upper lip where light-catching beads of water had formed, as if the internal pressures were forcing a protective layer of fluid to rise to the surface and ward off harm. I saw those beads and wanted to lick them away. His face looked hot. I wanted to test the heat with my mouth. But it was clear. He wanted me gone. He was terrified. I decided at once to leave as soon as I could get a flight. I would make the best of things. I would sightsee.

He dropped me at my hotel. I collapsed on the bed as if struck by a case of Victorian vapors. The shame of it all! I had wanted this trip to demonstrate my courage. I'd wanted a triumph of adult passion. And now that the worst possible outcome—rejection—had materialized, there was only one opportunity for mustering courage, and that would be in the face of failure.

I booked a flight for the next day. He took me to dinner at a noisy restaurant that night, precluding the threat of either romantic notions or serious conversation. He was about to make it through the day without sexual incident, and he drove me to the hotel, surely hoping that I would hop out and leave him to sigh in chaste relief. I turned to him and wanted to say, "What you have done is irresponsible and unforgivable."

Instead I sputtered, "What has this been about? All these years?" I must have been near tears.

He looked into his lap for a long while in silence, as if he were perhaps consulting his genitals, and then said, "I can't." He sighed. "You shouldn't have come." Then he looked up and took my hand, the first time since my arrival that he touched me. I was looking away. His hand was heavy on mine. "You'll get over it."

I shrugged free and got out of the car, slamming the door without looking back.

I managed to maintain my equilibrium during the flight home, but once I closed my apartment door, I cried off and on for several days, abashed and in mourning for the death of a dear old fantasy.

MANY YEARS PASSED. I was invited to the wedding of family friends. Because I had so thoroughly put Misha out of my mind by then, I never thought to ask who was invited. As I entered the hall I saw him from a distance. At the sight of him, a powerful fist of nausea clenched around my gut, as if I were the survivor of a terminal illness facing the threat of recurrence. He was dancing at the edge of the room, guiding a girl—and she *was* just a girl—smoothly across the floor. They stopped abruptly. Still holding her, he said something and led her to a corner. He seemed almost unchanged, actually improved by age, as if he had worked his charms on his maker, too, and had been rewarded with eternal youthfulness. He was dressed beautifully, as always, in a dark suit shaped to his still graceful form. Aging, on him, seemed theatrical and flashy, a form of enhancement. Only the hair had given way to time and was ribboned with brilliant stripes of silver. He looked like the young Ronald Colman done up with Hollywood shoe polish to play an older man. He was gesturing in the air as if telling a funny story. Suddenly, his mouth stilled. He leaned toward the girl and his profile disappeared into her hair. He was whispering and she, her hand cupped over her mouth, was giggling.

TWO

Gregory was drunk. He hadn't been for a long time. When he first met me, realizing he needed all his wits to capture and keep me, he quit drinking.

No, wait, that just sounds like rampant egomania. Try it again in a discreet Third Person.

When he first met Anna, realizing he needed all his wits to capture and keep her, he quit drinking. But that had been five years before, and even his outsized love and desperate need for her couldn't deter him from the bottle now.

Anna had been up late working. She was buoyed by the publication of her story in *The Atlantic Monthly* and was now continuing to write the narrative that the short story had unleashed in her, fictionalizing as she went along in an aloof third-person voice. When she finally retired that night, Gregory was in bed but still awake. He had a book in his hands but she could see that he was not reading. He looked rumpled and sour-faced and she knew immediately that he was not sober. Without saying a word, she walked around the bed to his side, took the glass of clear liquid that stood on his nighttable and sniffed it loudly. Gin, she thought, recoiling.

"Fine," she said pointedly, but to the air rather than to Gregory. She slipped into the bed and stayed as far to her side as possible, as if avoiding a contagion. She switched off her light. Gregory, still pretending to read, looked at her out of the side of his eye, saw that she was pretending to be asleep, took a gulp from his glass and turned off his light.

Anna woke up first, as usual. Five forty-five and only a dim light came through the windows. She sat up and stared at the man who had been lying in bed next to her every morning for the last five years. He'd rolled away with most of the covers during the night. Now she carefully loosened her half from his grip and pulled them up to her chin. The heat of his body and his hot, sleepy smell, something like a combination of fresh-baked bread and soggy gym socks, came off the fabric and filled her nostrils. Like a drug, the familiar odor was a comfort, a Pavlovian call back to happier times. But only the smell, separated from the man, was a comfort. Gregory, the actual person she lived with, the man in her bed, elicited an opposite reaction. She had recently found herself studying him when he wasn't looking, scrutinizing him critically as he chewed his meat, loaded his peas onto his fork, probed his gums for stray bits of food with his tongue. She watched him grimly as he put his pants on, as he adjusted his underwear, as he tied his shoes. All of these seemingly benign acts were slowly becoming indictable offenses in her eyes. He was drinking off and on and she knew that the end for them was near. She watched him now while he slept, when she was free to peer at him at length, looking for what it was that she once loved, for what had gone wrong. Gregory's face was stamped with wavering lines, the result of a nightlong battle to conquer his pillow. He looked as if he'd been lying on a printing press rather than a featherbed. The lines that had already been pressed into the skin by his ordinary and constant struggle with life seemed shallow in comparison. He had an imposingly handsome face, with broad, Slavic cheekbones that always made Anna imagine a violent Mongol invasion centuries back and the orgy of rape that must have followed, eventually producing Gregory, who, with his carved jaw, full, defiant lips and unflinching glare looked very much to be a blond, blue-eyed Asian warrior.

Now the pillow lay in submission crumpled under his heavy head. He was always doing battle these days, taking up arms against imagined enemies, Anna thought, herself a recent addition to the list of opponents.

She threw the covers off and went to the bathroom, where she caught her reflection in the mirror. She still looked all right. At thirty-two the brow was still miraculously unlined. Although when she was a girl she feared her features were excessively plain, she now liked her face, found it interesting enough. Her eyebrows were feathery eaves, graceful parentheses above her round, dark eyes. The bones around her eyes, at her jaw and in her neck were not prominent, but beneath her skin, skin that had a distinct and unusual shimmer, they were pleasantly discernible. Her bone structure faintly echoed her mother's stronger image. Anna had been told since she was young, and even she could now see, that her mouth looked ever ready to launch a kiss, lips slightly pursed, pushing forward into erotic space. The once ungovernable blue-black tresses had calmed themselves to sufficiently coalesce with the current fashion into something she could actually toss, like someone in a shampoo commercial. In male company she experienced a rush of power unleashed with that toss, as if the waves of moving hair—oceanic, slow-motion, mesmeric—communicated directly with men in a way that words could never compete. She thought her legs too thin, and so she hid them under trousers. The rest of her was slender but well formed. She was pleased by a general sense that she didn't take up much room.

Surely she could still attract a man. Surely she would not spend the rest of her life with a drunk. Surely Gregory could not embody the end of her romantic life.

WHEN GREGORY CAME to the kitchen, Anna was drinking coffee and reading the paper. His eyes looked small. He had cut himself shaving. Although he was showered and dressed, nothing could hide the fact that this was a man suffering the indignities and pain of a severe hangover.

As if he were an actor who had summoned the wherewithal to play a cheerful scene in spite of tragic personal setbacks, Gregory smiled widely at Anna. He saw a copy of the magazine and pointed to it heartily.

"They really did a great job illustrating your story. That costs money, hiring an artist. Shows real faith in your work." He studied the illustration with more than necessary concentration. "The girl even looks like those pictures of you when you were thirteen. You'll get an agent out of this, I'm sure."

Anna did not look up from the newspaper during this performance. "Maybe," was all she said.

Gregory was hurt by her coolness but not deterred. He knew the drinking probably had something to do with it so he didn't really want to ask what was bothering her. "I'm going to class," he said. Hearing no response or apparent interest in his plans, he continued. "Be back around two." Still nothing. "Don't shop. I'll pick up something for dinner. And I'll drop off the cleaning."

Still not looking at Gregory, Anna said, "I'm having lunch with Sydney. I'll be late."

Gregory's already concave face looked as if it had been rocked by an internal earthquake at this news, but he tried to conceal it. "Okay, see you later." He took his briefcase and left. Anna looked up as the door was closing and the telephone rang.

Her friend Dianne was on the other end.

"Hi. What's doing?"

"What's doing? I read your story."

"Oh. Well. That's good."

"Yeah, I liked it. It was good, but, just tell me, am I mixing it up with something else? This is the story that was the big secret?"

"Well, it's the story I told you about."

"So what's the secret? The same thing happened to me. My father's partner in the laundry. Every Thursday he came for dinner. And my sister, too, with our neighbor down the block. Always breathing down her neck. And my cousin Janie. Some high school teacher. That's your big secret, honey?"

She made a good point. Men are biologically programmed to be attracted to females whose physical assets promise high fertility, youth being the number-one asset. The history of the world is a chronicle of old men bedding young girls, of poor families selling attractive young daughters to ancient rich men, of kings taking girls as their queens, not to mention concubines. A fifty-year-old guy's gonads discern little difference between a twenty-one-year-old beauty and a thirteen-year-old in this context, even though society offers marriage to a trophy wife with regard to the former category and jail sentences regarding the latter. Only good manners, social mores and, in some cases, the police keep men from acting on this evolutionary hard-wiring. While matings between adolescent girls and older men might produce hearty offspring and assure the success of the species, the male attraction to youthful femininity matches up badly with the average thirteen-year-old's incapacity for dealing with the emotional complexities of a physical relationship. Too bad for the girls; given the strength of the male libido and the easy social mixing of older men and younger women, it would be a statistical anomaly if many girls were not being initiated by older men into sex—either suggested or actual—pretty damned often.

Every time a father has a sexual thought about his fifteen-year-old daughter's best friend but dismisses it, or a middle-aged clerk makes a flirtatious remark to a teenage customer but goes no further, social disapproval is doing its work. Under the tyranny of testosterone, for some mature men, saying no to temptation is probably as common as struggling to live in monogamy. The trouble is not all men say no.

THREE

Sonia was sitting at the kitchen table with Max. She held *The Atlantic* in her hand as she read Anna's story.

Max put down his coffee cup. His cheeks were sucked in close to his facial bones. Sonia knew this look; it signaled grave displeasure.

"Do you think it's true?"

"I don't know."

"You don't know?" He shook his head. "We've known him, how long? Forty years? What if it's true? How could he do this to us? To her. Our daughter."

Sonia was looking into her plate at the toast she wasn't eating. She spoke, but without conviction.

"She's a writer. She makes things up."

"You think that's all?"

"I'm sure." Sure? Sonia knew about Boston. Someone knew someone who knew someone else who knew Misha and that someone saw Anna at the Boston airport being picked up. Perhaps there was an innocent explanation. Over the years, whenever her suspicions were raised, she had found ways to dismiss them. After all, in her youth she had nearly married him. He could have been Anna's father. He was her friend. Max's friend.

"Did you invite him to the party?" Max asked.

"Of course. How could I not? A seventieth birthday. He would hear about it. He came to the sixtieth."

Max grunted. "Ten years ago I was still speaking to him."

"Twenty minutes ago you were still speaking to him."

Max said nothing for several seconds. He was thinking of how he had managed to maintain a friendship with a man whose character he'd always known to be dubious. During the war Misha was a great provider of diversion. Max enjoyed the irreverent company. They made illegal alcohol together. They hid in ditches to evade hard-labor assignments. Misha was a rule breaker—not out of philosophical conviction like Max, but rather from lack of self-control. Max and Misha discovered common ground the way an antiwar protester of the nineteen sixties and a juvenile delinquent might. Both could be found throwing rocks or breaking into the occasional Selective Service office, but for completely different reasons.

Max knew he had bested a rival when he won Sonia's heart. Misha, the ultimate irresponsible, had actually asked Sonia to marry him. She told Max that she was never in love with Misha, only infatuated as a girl of seventeen—there was something about a first kiss—but maturity soon opened her eyes to who he was. They had never slept together. Max believed her, particularly because she refused, on a regular basis, to sleep with Max during their long courtship. In the Kovno ghetto, jealous Jewish women well past their prime were forever accusing attractive young women of consorting with the enemy. These unfortunate victims were then forced to undergo a humiliating examination of the state of their hymens. Those whose hymens were deemed insufficiently intact were punished severely. Besides, after 1942, pregnancy was forbidden. Pregnant Jewish women were put to death. Sonia, a big believer in the human capacity for brutality, was intent on being prepared for the worst-case scenario. So although Max accepted Sonia's story, he nevertheless always treated Misha with special care. After the liberation, Misha's behavior made it clear that the effort to divert himself from the horrors of the war was actually just a convenient expression of his true nature. Peacetime didn't flatter him.

There were women. There was drinking. Max's preference would have been to see him as infrequently as possible and thank god Misha lived in Boston, several hours away, but Sonia seemed to retain a sentimental attachment. Misha flirted with her, harmlessly Max was sure, and it made Sonia feel good, so how could he deny her? Still, he always kept his eyes open.

"You're not going to make a scene."

"Do I ever make a scene?"

There was another silence. Max finally spoke.

"Do you consider murder a scene?"

"Ha," said Sonia. She sighed and reread the first page of the story.

"Frankly, I'm more worried about Gregory than this story."

Sonia looked up.

"I think we made a mistake disapproving of him so strongly. She's afraid to talk to us about him now. I worry he's drinking again. I worry she stays with him just because we disapprove."

"Too embarrassing to admit we were right?"

Sonia nodded.

"I think she'll leave him," he said out of hope more than knowledge. "How long could she live with that."

"So? Is it?" Sydney was waving the magazine at Anna.

"Is what what?"

"Is the story true? Is this piece an actual account of some unrepentant *mitteleuropean* lecher tampering with a minor while her parents fiddled? Or did you make it up?"

"From you of all people this question? What do *you* say when *Time* magazine calls to ask if you are the sexually adventurous hero of your picaresque novel, *Younger Women*?"

"I don't give interviews. And I *am*. Everyone knows that." Sydney pushed his reading glasses back along the bumpy ridge of his nose, raised his eyebrows to settle the glasses and looked down on Anna. She was sitting in a threadbare easy chair in his study, drinking the coffee he had made her, hoping he would drop the background check and get around to discussing the story's merits, and lauding them.

"What is this thing of yours for older men?"

"Listen, you and I both know I wouldn't be here right now chatting if I didn't have some problem in that area. And we wouldn't be here either if you weren't, let's say, susceptible to the charms of younger women."

"Your second premise is granted, but are you saying you and I are friends only because of my age?"

"Can we change the subject?"

Sydney shifted in his seat and smiled wickedly.

"So you really didn't sleep with him?"

Anna sighed. "I find that when the conversation turns to sex, it usually signals the onset of a come-on."

"My reasons are purely scientific. Research for my next book."

"So you're not working your way to a proposition?"

They had fallen into the habit of skewering each other verbally, the pretense being that their closeness allowed them to merrily fling cold insults without inflicting or sustaining any injuries. Anna would mock his record on marriage, referring to Sydney's four wives by their numerical ranking in the Aronson chronology, to put a distance between herself and the prospect of romance with Sydney. Also, while Sydney's marriages were fraught with friction and pain and the irrationality spawned by unmet expectations, her relationship with Sydney was calm, felicitous and characterized by extreme courtesy and thoughtfulness. She thought herself several rungs above his wives in Sydney's esteem. She placed herself in a realm safe from the malaise of marriage and the symptoms that go with it.

Also, the bantering was part of her Scheherazade act. She wanted more than anything to be Sydney's most entertaining liaison. She feared he might disappear if she failed to be diverting, and she depended on his being there. She, in fact, needed him. So instead of having a real conversation they had an Abbott and Costello routine.

She could see from his expanding diaphragm that he had a good line prepared. "Ah," he said, taking a cheerful breath, an infusion of gusto, "at this point in our friendship a proposition would be an unforgivable lapse. But let me point out that it *is* interesting that you've found such a transcendental meeting of the minds with someone—me—who happens to be old enough to be your father."

"I'm not looking for another father. That position is currently filled."

"Okay, enough." Sydney pointed to the magazine. "I don't want to be your father. How about editor? Why didn't you show the story to me? All those adjectives."

Anna defended herself. "I knew you'd pick it to pieces. I'd already written a dozen drafts. *You* might enjoy spending eleven years on a story before submitting it but I had hoped to be published some time before menopause."

"I'm not that bad."

"It's funny. When I first met you nothing would have made me happier than to have you read my work."

The first time she met Sydney, six years earlier, she had wanted very much to show him her work but assumed that everyone he encountered had a manuscript to spring on him. After she finished at the University of Chicago, she would hang around the bookstore owned by Foster Krasny, a man whose fame derived chiefly from being Sydney's friend, hoping to catch sight of the great writer whose work had so inspired her. After about six months without result, coming to the bookstore had become part of her routine, unrelated to her original mission. She was now a habitué rather than a would-be celebrity watcher. The clerks nodded when she entered, not exactly friendly but as if to acknowledge the percentage of their salaries her regular purchases subsidized. Then, one day, there was Sydney Aronson at a table in the back, dwarfed behind high stacks of his latest book, a book she had bought the first day it was out and had read in one sitting. He was scribbling in the books, methodically taking one from the pile of the unsigned, peering through his reading glasses, half-moons hooked over his beak, and slowly forming his even and measured scrawl, the same as in the last book, the same as the next. As he wrote, his host, the frenetic Krasny, behaved as if the pope had dropped in. He couldn't seem to do enough for Sydney. Krasny prowled the store, hunched like a sherpa guide longing to offer directions or help with a heavy load. He ached to be essential but clearly no one needed him at that moment. He wore reading glasses but he wasn't reading. He muttered pleasantries but no one was listening. He paced as if his cautious steps constituted detail work rather than an expression of his anxiety. He fretted, ever mindful of his prestigious guest's comfort. But Sydney was signing the books and needed no assistance. "Here are more pens, Syd," he said, almost bowing with the weight of his admiration. Krasny wiggled a pillow between Sydney and his chair to ease a chronically painful back, and seemed proud to be so well acquainted with the famous back's ailment.

They'd done this book-signing bit together before, Anna could see. While Krasny hovered, Sydney blithely continued to reproduce his smooth cursive in book after book with pressureless ease, the effort not even whitening his knuckles. His serenity made Krasny's busy flitting seem all the more ridiculous. Sydney only looked up to keep the piles straight. He shouldn't be doing it, Anna thought while watching him from the nearby stacks. If he should form letters at all they should be the fundaments of fictions. A book-signing is what Jackie Collins does. Perhaps he thinks he is doing it for his old friend Krasny, who seems to smugly enjoy the traffic through the store and the prestige the Aronson imprimatur confers. Even Sydney's posture longed for more substantial composition. His spine was rolled out to full extension, his neck straight up, his jaw cocked to give him the angle through the tilted glasses. Simply writing his name, he had the look of someone in the act of creation.

Anna had seen him briefly the previous night at a dinner honoring him. She caught sight of him through crowds of people seeking to shake his hand, to congratulate him on his new publication and to clap him on the back for winning the minor local award that launched the evening at a hotel ballroom. She was struck by his physical clarity. He was fifty-nine years old, she had just read somewhere, but his face had lost none of its sharpness. It had not yet been redefined by gravity. Its contours and planes rose and fell at their own pleasure rather than under the dictates of natural forces. Did he look old? a friend later asked her. An objective reply would have taken into account the long creases that radiated from the corners of his heavily lidded eyes, the tiny fissures in his lips, the loosened forehead skin. He was certainly fifty-nine years old but he still had a facial vigor, a Ray

Bolger, Joe DiMaggio puss, honed and edgy like the blade of a tomahawk, protrusive in profile, a sliver head on. A smile would crack his face into accordion shafts, neat economical folds. At first look she could easily see the young man who once existed beneath the patina of age. In fact, that was all she could see. She was not persuaded by the collapsed, dented visage, its horizons expanded by a hairline in retreat. His wrinkles couldn't deny an odor of desire about him. He was still brimming with want and fueled by a knowledge that the want could be fulfilled because he had always been, and still was, so strangely good-looking.

She gathered her courage and emerged from the stacks. "Does it cost more with a signature?" she asked. Krasny responded first, humorlessly, ever the earnest sherpa. "No, it's the same price."

"It's more with a complete set of fingerprints," Sydney said, taking the bait enthusiastically. He looked up from the books to see a dark-haired, black-eyed supplicant. Immediately he wanted to know her.

"I was at the dinner for you last night," she said, unable to think of anything else. "I'm afraid I thought those speeches praising your virtues would never end. But I did enjoy your talk."

"Well, I have many virtues. But thank you anyway. And what is your name?"

The night before in his speech, he had told of famous writers he'd met in his youth. "He didn't know he was being met by me," Sydney joked of his introduction to Sinclair Lewis. Apparently the besotted Lewis liked to swat young writers down. "Don't tell me your name," Lewis would say. "I'll never remember."

"Anna Schopenhauer," she said, remembering Lewis.

"Are you German? Of Dutch extraction, that is?"

She laughed. "Hardly. Lithuanian. We're Lithuanian."

"Lithuanian Jewish? Or plain?"

"Jewish. By some genealogical wrong turn we ended up with that name. I don't know how."

"You have an interesting accent. Must be Western Lithuanian. Like maybe New York City?"

"Well, yes, I was born in this country . . ."

"So why do you call yourself Lithuanian?"

Flustered, Anna tried to explain. "You asked if I was Dutch. I thought . . . My parents . . ."

"When did they get here?"

"After the war."

"Which one?"

"The second."

Sydney waited for more information.

"World."

"They were in a camp?"

"No. A ghetto. Kovno."

"Kovno was burned. How did they survive?"

"They escaped. A guard tipped them."

"They were lucky."

"Yes."

"Lucky for you. Well, maybe not. How do I know? So with a name like Schopenhauer, are you a philosopher?"

"No. I write about theater and books for the *Chicago Bird*. I used to be freelance. Now I'm on staff. Almost making a living."

"And you're writing a novel?"

She was blushing. "Well, yes, trying to."

"You've got a very good name. The usual spelling?" Anna nodded. He looked at her appreciatively for a moment, then opened to the flyleaf of a fresh book and wrote. "There." He handed over the book. "Is that good enough, or should I try another?"

"Fine, yes," Anna said as, politely feigning gratitude, she took the offered book now imprinted with her name and Sydney Aronson's together. She realized at that moment that the price for meeting Sydney was buying a signed eighteen-ninety-five book that she already owned.

Krasny interrupted their moment of silent eye contact. "The book is selling like crazy, Syd. You should be very happy. A quality book that actually sells. Today everything is schlock. Everything is so shoddy. Writing, everything. No one writes like you, Syd. You and your quality stuff." Sydney laughed and signed another book.

Krasny was dancing around the pair, sensing an attraction between them that would surely bubble up to the surface were he not so vigilant a chaperone. "Did you see this?" Krasny held up a copy of the latest *New York Times Book Review* to Anna, the cover featuring a photograph of a demurely reclining Sydney surrounded by the profuse praise of another novelist who no doubt hoped some other novelist-reviewer would do the same for him one day.

"This one is really well written," Krasny carried on. "It's all positive, nothing in there that should bother you, eh Syd?"

"I don't think that is generally the criterion on which to judge criticism, Foster."

"But those reviews of the last book, all those terrible reviews, they weren't even of the book. They were of you. By your enemies. They had a field day."

It was true that the last book was not as rich as Sydney's earlier work. Sydney's writing was so clean and dense—the product, Anna surmised, of obsessive and interminable reworking, art that had traveled as far as human effort could propel it. Then came the alchemy, she assumed, the incantations. She imagined Sydney laying out the pages in the sun, to evaporate every unnecessary syllable from out of the manuscript, leaving only the distilled essentials, a potent, concentrated prose. He hadn't, she felt, left the last book out to dry long enough.

"Well," Anna ventured, hoping to drop a friendship-cementing profundity, "It's an incestuous line of work, book reviewing. With novelists competing . . ."

"*I've* never committed incest," Sydney said, laughing at her. "I have been denied my opportunities. Have you, Ms. Schopenhauer?"

She could feel her face redden as he went on. "No incest for me," he said again. He was standing now, grinning. She had amused him. She examined his mouth. His teeth were long and discolored but they didn't offend. His mammoth charm overran all shortcomings. He became jaunty as he denied his experience with incest. It was a prolonged good humor. Krasny seemed to feel left out and envious of Anna's success with Sydney. To win back his supremacy, he began to laugh more loudly than Sydney. Sydney, however, was oblivious to the ploy. Sydney was letting loose. His shoulders were shuddering as he laughed. His voice went higher. "I have been robbed of all my opportunities," he repeated. He was on the balls of his feet. He was fifty years old, then forty, then thirty, all energy and spunk. Not that he found incest so amusing. But how nice and unexpected it was that he was laughing with a pretty woman, when only a minute ago Sydney was being forced to mourn the era's literary paucity.

Krasny was trying to regain control of the situation that had slipped from his sovereignty, the undivided attention of Sydney he had just recently presided over. "Aren't you going to sign any more? They're going like hotcakes."

"Presumably people are buying the book for all the stuff that comes *after* the signature, Foster."

"Yeah, but it's a nice touch, your name in the front. And you're not going to live forever, Syd."

LATER, AS ANNA was reluctantly paying for her forced purchase, Krasny came up behind her at the register and whispered so closely in her ear that she could feel his words delivered in a warm mist mixed with the smell of spirits.

"Aren't you lucky?" he said. Then he grabbed her by the shoulders and gave her a rude and wet kiss that missed her cheek and smeared off along her jaw.

HOW DID THE friendship grow? They had coffee that afternoon and saw a movie a few days later, and now Sydney was acting wounded that Anna would publish a story without consulting him first.

"And another thing. I could have gotten you more money for the piece. You should have let my agent handle it for you. What did they pay you?"

"Your agent wouldn't take me on. Ten percent of nothing is nothing. Anyway, money wasn't the point."

"I see you'll never be a great writer."

"Someone already wants to make a movie out of it."

"From this story? It's pretty slender."

"The producer called it 'explosive.' "

"I hope that was *his* word."

"It was. I said I didn't think it was terribly explosive but as long as you're making a movie out of it I could use the money. Then he told me he didn't really have any money but he was positive he could raise some if I would just sell him a six-month option for two-ninety-eight."

"What films has he made?"

Anna laughed. "He hasn't exactly made any."

"If this impoverished producer manqué manages to make a movie out of your story, there will be publicity and some reporter will eventually ask if that story, and it's in a perfectly reputable publication, though not as good as *The New Yorker* . . ."

"What, only some rag would publish me?"

He rapped the magazine on the table for her attention.

"Anna. There will be publicity. Speculation."

"I think you're being a little overdramatic. Who would care about this?"

"You're talking about a story in a national publication in which a grown man has his way with a thirteen-year-old. Sexually. For chrissakes, they banned *Lolita*. This is just *Lolita* from the girl's point of view. It's about a Lolita in the eye of the beholder. And they never even screw. It's more a case of psychological abuse. So much the better for purposes of titillation."

She was drifting away, lost in the mesmerizing thought that her prose might someday be confused with Nabokov's. That was some leap, she thought, from her tale of unrequited lust to the story of a cockteaser and a madman.

"I love you. You get cranky when you're feeling protective," Anna said.

"Don't patronize me."

"Can we talk about something else?"

"Have you heard from the guy in the story? What's his name? Misha?"

"It's fiction."

"You're going to hear from him. You understand that."

"God, no. I haven't seen him in ten years."

"Well, you've certainly sent out an all-points bulletin. He'll call."

"That would be absurd."

"You're not over him, are you? I'm jealous."

"There's nothing to be over."

"Maybe not, but he's bound to call."

"He wouldn't dare. Really. It's been ten years."

"Anyway, won't you see him back in New York for your father's seventieth birthday?"

"Can we talk about something else?"

"You pick."

"I'm tired. How about a moment of silence?"

"How's Gregory?"

"This isn't such a hot subject, either."

"What's wrong?"

"It's too much to go into now. How's your wife?"

"Things must be bad if you're asking after Sally's health. Oh, I know what we can talk about. Why aren't we sleeping together?"

"That was a pretty smooth transition. Very suave."

"Suave hasn't worked with you. I'm trying a new approach."

"You're too old for me," Anna said.

"I'm younger than that flaky swain in your story."

"It's fiction, Sydney."

"But I'm not. I'm flesh. I'm blood. I'm distinguished-looking. And you love bow ties."

She did, in fact, think him attractive, in spite of the bow ties. "I've reformed."

"Really? You're like an ex-smoker dying to light up and here is your favorite brand sitting on the table right in front of you. One day you'll fall in love with me and we'll run away together."

"What would your wife say?"

"As a scientist, she would treat our union as a fortuitous opportunity for observation of human sexual behavior. She'd probably enjoy measuring the frequency and duration of our couplings. Use it to write one of her indecipherable monographs. She'd consider it a favor." He removed his glasses and, as he smiled, his face folded into a portfolio of flaps and creases. "I have to say I would never have believed that of all the people who have come knocking at my door, of all the fame freaks and unpublished kooks and hangers-on and aspiring biography writers and academic schmoozers who have attempted to get close, that it would be to a sexual degenerate nearly three decades my junior to whom I would end up serving coffee on a regular basis. It seems an amazing feat of specifically designed punitive retribution by a supposedly nonintervening god—which is the only kind I believe in—to go to the trouble to arrange. How did I end up with you as a best friend?"

"You like sexual malcontents. We give you something to write about."

"True."

"We talked about incest the first time we met. That should have been a tip-off, I think."

"Speaking of incest, have your parents read it?"

"That's a hell of a crack and no, I haven't spoken to them about it yet."

"They'll know this guy, won't they? And it won't raise his status in their eyes any, I presume."

"I'll say I made it up."

"So you didn't," he said triumphantly. Sydney stood up and straightened the creases in his pants. "What *is* it with you and older men?" He held out his hand to her. "I'm starving. Let's have lunch at George's. We'll take a table up front. I want everyone to know that we're having an affair."

THE LATE TWENTIETH CENTURY

FOUR

The smell of stale coffee and old cigarettes permeated Anna's cubicle at work. She didn't drink coffee or smoke; the smells were left to her by previous occupants, and they reminded her every day that one day she, too, might be a previous occupant, if she got lucky.

She picked up the ringing telephone and said, "Hello."

Gregory was on the other end, sounding baleful and repentant.

"No, I'll pick something up," she said. "Are you having solids today?"

"I'm not drunk."

"No, you don't sound drunk."

"Well, you should be glad, not sarcastic."

"I am glad. It's just a little difficult to work up much enthusiasm for your intermittent sobriety. I mean, it's such an erratic and fleeting condition with you."

"I'm sorry."

"I know you're sorry."

"I love you."

"I love you, too."

"See you later."

Anna hung up and sighed. Why can't it be the way it used to be, she wondered.

On their first date everything seemed so promising. They dined at a restaurant whose hanging ferns had been too well tended by a gifted green thumb. It was the romantic destination of the moment, and the teeming vegetation was meant to convey lushness, fertility. Gregory was telling Anna one of his many stories.

"He was this strange guy who never washed his hair. A kind of Raskolnikov. I thought if he hadn't already murdered some old woman, he was going to one day soon. I gave him an A just so I'd never have to have a tutorial with him again."

Their young waiter, though not covered with ferns, had a well-gardened look about him, too. His face burst forth with what seemed a newly planted beard.

"Is everything all right?"

"Fine, thanks," said Gregory.

"Can I get you anything else to drink? Wine?"

"Not for me. Anna?"

Anna said no and the waiter left them.

"Have you been here before?" Gregory asked.

"No, this is my first time. Do you come here?"

"No. My first time, too. I like it. Let's come back."

"I was surprised you called," Anna said.

"I enjoyed our interview. It was fun talking to you. I teach literature, but I don't actually get to talk about literature very often. I don't think many of my students would know who Raskolnikov is."

"So you called to talk about literature?"

"No. I liked you when you came to see me before the opening. You actually asked me intelligent questions. I expected a routine session with a dopey journalist and you surprised me. I felt a real connection with you."

Anna blushed.

"I'm sorry. I don't mean to embarrass you. If you get embarrassed at compliments you'll just have to endure a few more moments of blushing. Because I also couldn't help but notice that you were wonderful to look at. I'm sorry. I'm making you blush a deeper scarlet. If it's any consolation, you look spectacular in red."

"Thank you," she managed.

"Anyway, I couldn't really call you until after you reviewed my play. For one thing, I didn't want to be accused of influencing your opinion. And besides, of course, I wanted to be sure that you recognized what a genius I am. You wouldn't believe the astonishingly high number of people who remain ignorant of my genius. You're an exceptional woman."

"So you never go out with anyone who doesn't think you're a genius?"

"Life is already an obstacle course of arbitrary friction and uncertainty. And self-doubt? I have enough for several selves. I like to be surrounded by people who are sure. Sure of my talent. I prefer the company of people with a firm grip on reality."

"So my good review proved that I wasn't living in a dream world?"

"You're not, are you?"

"I don't know. I think I'm pretty rooted in reality, but I could just be imagining that."

"I think you're the most rooted woman I've ever met."

Anna blushed again, trying to ignore Gregory's last remark.

"I mean that in the nicest possible way."

They sat in silence for several seconds.

"Do you think everyone in this room thinks I'm your father?"

"How old *are* you?"

"Forty-seven. And you?"

"Twenty-seven. Anyway, I would find it hard to believe that you haven't dated students now and then. Younger than I."

"Yes, but we never actually had conversations. I went to bed with them. We talked about how they might have done better on an exam. Our literary interests coincided only when we read the instructions off the back of the spermicide tube together."

Gregory laughed at his own joke. In another man, Anna might have found this off-putting, but Gregory's delight in himself lifted her spirits. His laugh rolled out of his mouth—through his wide smile, through lips almost feminine in their redness. She imagined them smiling up against her own lips.

"I'll just bet you're a big believer in marriage," Anna said.

"I've had two wives. Not a very good record."

"You sound like you're boasting."

"No, just declaring the contents of my baggage. Have you ever been married?"

"No. Never believed in it. Even when they're good in the beginning, how can that hormonally induced euphoria possibly be expected to last?"

"Marriage is a very good thing," Gregory said with surprising seriousness. Anna's left hand was curved around the base of her water glass. Gregory reached for it, moving aside the glass.

"Your hands are beautiful," he said, sliding his fingers up her delicate bones. "A ring would look nice here." He lifted her hand and rested it on his, palm to palm. His hand was warm. Anna allowed it to stay. Her heart sped up momentarily and she found it difficult to swallow. She withdrew her hand and said, "So why did your marriages end?"

Gregory looked at his empty palm and closed it. He smiled.

"Why? You may not believe this, but I didn't behave very well. But that's a story for another dinner."

Looking back, Anna realized that Gregory might as well have told her everything about himself. It wouldn't have stopped her.

"You know, I'm really the perfect man for you. I'm arrogant and flamboyant in a kind of shy, Midwestern, embarrassed-that-

I'm-not-from-New-York way. I'm on the wagon now, and I can be an impossible drunk if things aren't going exactly my way. But for you, I'll quit drinking for years at a time. I'm passionate and loyal and I could fall madly in love with you. I'm also well known around here for my artistic integrity, just the sort of thing you admire. I never write anything that has the least hope of making money. Actors love to speak my lines, and critics love to explain their deeper meaning. Audiences wonder what the fuck I'm talking about but they don't mind because they just assume I'm talking over their heads and that it must therefore be art. I'll never make a living at it, which is why I have to teach freshman English to illiterates. And I'm not Jewish, so your parents will hate me."

But what he really said was far less helpful.

"Your parents must hate that you left New York for Chicago."

"Yes, they do. But I go back to visit pretty often. I was just there for my father's sixty-fifth birthday. Big party. The Litvaks—Lithuanians, that is—they all came to the United States after the war. They're always looking for an excuse to sing sad songs and drink vodka and eat dense food. Kreplach, dumplings, gefilte fish, meat loaf. Everything they eat has such mass. And it all reminds them of the old days, and that reminds me of the war. Funny. I suppose I associate dense food with death. Considering the way you feel after eating a matzo ball, I guess it's no wonder."

"Well, I'd love to cook you some nice dense food myself. I can give you everything but the vodka. Why don't you come over Friday?"

"I'd love to."

No, it wouldn't have stopped her.

FIVE

Suddenly I was up in the air. Reading Anna's story makes me think of it. Of the time I saw Misha after the war. One minute I was walking down the street, just glad to be alive. It was the week after the liberation. Even just breathing in and out was thrilling, full of romance and promise, like popping a champagne cork. And the next minute someone is lifting me from the ground and twirling me and shouting, "Sonia! You're alive! You're not dead! Let's get married!"

He put me down and stood back, hands on his hips, taking me in, looking me over the way he always did. "You're thin, but you're not ruined." I could have kicked him. I knew I looked awful. Well dressed, but awful anyway. He, on the other hand, looked as if nothing so inconvenient as a war had ever troubled him. He was clean-shaven. He smelled good. He'd found a razor, soap. He had access to water. His clothes looked not only clean but new. He'd been making deals. Max and I and everyone we knew were struggling.

He was as attractive as ever.

"I thought you were dead," he said.

"Of course. What else? We all think everyone is dead," I

said. "Until we see them. It will probably go on like this for the rest of our lives. Running into ghosts."

"Yes, but I don't want to marry everyone I run into."

"Don't be ridiculous," I said, but I was already laughing. That was what Misha could do to you. I was nineteen years old and susceptible.

"Come on. Let's get married."

"Again? Have you asked anyone else to marry you today?"

"No. Only you, Sonia. It's you I always loved."

"Misha, you think I'm one of the stupid ones you seduce?"

Even as I spoke I admit I felt a slight twinge of jealousy for all the "stupid ones." Not sensible jealousy, not envy for what they had with Misha. I never really wanted him, not seriously, but that slight twinge was there anyway, even behind the dismissal that more truly represented my feelings towards him.

"Anyway, I'm married."

"To who?"

"To Max."

"That bum?"

Misha and "that bum" were close friends and drinking buddies. They had often been cell mates after arrests for misfired black-marketing schemes. I heard Misha had lost his wife and child. The wife had been more rich than pretty and was a few years older than he. Maybe the wisdom of age gave her the patience to put up with his flirtations. Basia could have done better—with all her money—but Misha was fun and charming and full of nervous energy and projects and plans, and when he turned his attentions on you you felt you were the only one. Maybe Basia died before she figured out how indiscreet he had really been.

I was thirteen years old the first time I met him, in 1939. My mother had died shortly after sending me to what she thought was safety, across the Polish border to unoccupied Lithuania. Misha was a handsome twenty-three-year-old, far too old for me but interesting nevertheless. I had seen him in his prime, when he'd have a new woman every night. I was the youngest in our crowd—I always had older friends—and I was so naïve. In the beginning I hardly knew what it was that he and all those willing victims were doing out there after curfew in his dark trysting spots. I saw the girls returning from "dates" with him, their hair rearranged from the way it had looked earlier in the evening, their clothing twisted and rebuttoned. One after another after another. Even then I could see what sex meant to him. Sex was like a hard-boiled egg. You're hungry, you eat it, it's gone, and you forget about that specific, undistinguished hard-boiled egg.

When I was fifteen I was working in the office of the delousing station with some older women—they were probably eighteen, maybe twenty. Misha used to come around after his shift inside the station just as we were finishing, doing his best to lure one of them into being that evening's sexual amusement. He usually had a flask in his pocket full of some lethal potion and he'd offer drinks all around. One evening, after he'd already had a few and while he was waiting for Maya, a pretty nineteen-year-old stenographer, he managed to steal a kiss from me. I'd kissed a boy before, Yulik, but we were both thirteen. Misha was the first *man* I'd kissed, and it was a different kind of a kiss. I slapped him and ran away. But I saw him every day for the next year or so and, briefly, when I was about seventeen, we were, sort of, boyfriend and girlfriend. He asked me to marry him. I actually thought about it, stupid as I was. Then a friend asked me, "Why are you running around with that Misha? He has a wife and a baby." This was the cause of the second slap. But he just said to me, "We'll all be dead tomorrow. Let's live now. I love you. I can't help that I have a wife. Hitler will kill all of us anyway. Do you want to die a virgin?"

I said, "If the choice is dying a virgin or sleeping with you, I'll take my chances." And we both started to laugh.

SIX

Celia's breasts, the thought of which could usually distract him long-distance, over the telephone or from across town, now were right there next to him in bed, within arm's reach. A short grab. But they held no allure, no promise of lulling comfort for Misha.

He would love to have been lost in them, but he was thinking of another woman and other anatomical parts. He was thinking of Anna and cutting her heart out, and of his wife, Angel, who would be difficult to calm after she read this story Anna had so impolitely written. Reading the story would be Angel's first literary endeavor in a long time, but the Lithuanian grapevine would be sure to casually hint to her that there might be something of particular interest in the latest *Atlantic Monthly*. It would take weeks before she would speak to him again and certainly she would throw something at him first. Something breakable. Something of his. If only she were staying at their place in Palm Beach she might never know anything about this moment in the history of Lithuanian gossip. In Boston, she was sure to hear of it soon.

Celia rolled over and put Misha's hand on her right breast.

He made the effort to respond but it was a response without truth. Can you *feel* a lie? he wondered, scanning her face for a sign of accusation. Celia, meaty and aromatic like a heavy stew, on other occasions possessed the capacity to make him forget his name. Now he couldn't remember how that could possibly be. Angel might want a divorce. Oh, there had been dalliances before, but nothing so public. No, she'd reconsider. Who would marry her now? She had become dried-out and bloated. The delicate girl he had married twenty-one years before was difficult to discern beneath the pastry-fed tiers of added flesh; there was too much extra for him to attempt exploratory excavation. She must have stopped wanting him, he thought, when she learned of his fling with an old friend, the wife of a Boston banker. Now Angel was fat and spent. She hid herself half the year in the Palm Beach retreat that her father's money had paid for. Misha's efforts and his genius for customer relations had turned her father's thriving business into a gold mine. He had earned his keep, all right, and the work he did allowed him to maintain his self-respect, but basically he was a kept man with a girlfriend on the side; a lapdog with a pet hamster.

He and Angel lived almost separately as it was, and when their paths crossed at one of their homes she didn't seem to have any desire for his physical attentions. So he was left to pursue his interests discreetly. But now a national magazine was chronicling many years of indiscretion. How did this happen?

Celia was rubbing his chest. You won't be too fond of me, either, when you hear this one, he thought, looking at her. How could she start the story when she was *thirteen*? Fortunately, Misha had plenty of time before he had to worry about Celia's reaction to the story. Celia was another one who wasn't a great reader, and certainly not of literary magazines. They probably subscribed to that magazine in the doctor's office where she worked—Celia was his cardiologist's nurse. He was due there soon for a checkup. Maybe he could steal that issue. Why had Anna made the portrait so vivid? And why did she paint him such a villain? They were consenting adults. All right, not adults, but consenting. She enjoyed it. What was the harm? What did he do, after all? Eventually some man, or boy, would do what he did. That's how young women learn about life. What was the harm?

But the more critical question for now was, What was he going to say? To Angel? To Celia? To Sonia? He would say it never happened. "Why would I? There are so many girls out there."

If I *had* done something it might have been just to make a girl feel important, confident, so that she would know that one day, men would want her and do for her the things that I, at my age, far too old of course, couldn't. What would be wrong with that? *If* I had done anything, anything that meant anything. Which of course I didn't.

Why this vindictive account? Could they have paid her for that trash? If she needed money she could have come to him. Of course, he hadn't seen her in years. From her parents he had received occasional reports. They knew, particularly Sonia, that he had always found Anna "special," as he would put it, carefully avoiding specifics. She was a charming girl, a blusher. Who could resist? But Sonia couldn't have known how far he had taken it and she wouldn't be pleased to find out. More than the wrath of Angel or Celia, he worried about hurting Sonia. After all, it was the reminder of the young Sonia that drew him to Anna. Now poor Sonia would read the story and probably feel that she loosed Anna unknowingly into the hands of a maniac, he thought, and after wallowing in that guilt, Sonia would feel rejected by him and, worst of all, old. There a time when *Sonia* used to blush in my presence, he thought, and I couldn't resist her then either. We had some good times. Maybe I even loved her. We'll have to talk. I'll let her yell at me, then maybe she'll hit me, too, and I'll give her a hug and we'll be old friends again. It's not so terrible. Her daughter didn't go crazy because of me. She isn't a lesbian or a bank robber or a heroin addict. As far as he knew, she was perfectly normal and functional.

He only wished she'd had a little less success with her writing career. Why couldn't she be one of those advertising people with a short story in the drawer that stayed in the drawer? How did she get that thing published? It wasn't very good. Was she sleeping with the publisher?

Celia had stepped up her ministrations. His eyes were closed. She was working on him with her amazing mouth but to no avail. He had a deflation, a vacuum, a black hole. He felt his parts turning away from her and crawling inward, retreating into his own canals and passages. He opened his eyes. I will end up with only myself still talking to me, he thought.

"Anna?"

She knew that voice. "Yes?"

Sydney had warned her. "I hope you know that this story will rouse the star of the narrative."

So with Sydney's prediction in her memory she listened to the voice. The telephone was a weight in her hand.

"It's Misha," the voice said.

She thought of replying "Misha who?" but she couldn't organize her tongue to perpetrate the slight.

"I guess it's been a long time," he said. She still hadn't spoken. "Ten years, I think." He waited for some sound, some sign, some sort of participation, but heard nothing. "Are you there?"

"Yes. I don't know."

"I read your story." He hoped she would say, "Well, now

you know how I felt. Now you know what a shit you are," but she didn't speak. "It was very good," he said.

"You're talking about its literary merits?" She was nearly sputtering.

"Yes, I mean, it had a lot of feeling. The way you describe things."

"You're calling to offer a critical assessment?"

"No, I just called to say that I understand how you must have felt. I see now what it must have looked like to you, how you must have seen it."

"Seen what?"

She wasn't going to let him off easily, he could see. She was angrier than he'd expected. There would be no chance to explain to her how much trouble she was causing him. He tried again.

"After reading the story, I can see how you must have looked at me, but I don't think I was really that insensitive."

"I presume that you're talking about 'Funny Accent,' and it's fiction. It's not about you." Anna's hands were shaking. He thinks I should apologize for having written the story? "Look, it's nice of you to call. Thank you for thinking of me. I have to go now. I think that after all these years you understand that I neither want to see you nor talk to you. Please don't call again."

"I just wanted to tell you that I'm making a special trip to your father's . . ." but she had hung up.

He would be seeing her soon.

SEVEN

For a long time Anna and Gregory felt they were the happiest couple they knew. They loved each other. They spent all their time together. He worked on his plays. She worked on a novel. They were exceedingly courteous and accommodating of each other's whims. They laughed. They cooked. With great effort Gregory remained sober. Life was good.

And that's the wonder of it. Two people who have no business being together for more than five minutes in casual conversation mistake charming locutions and momentary entertainment for signs of ultimate compatibility. How simultaneously funny and sad that people who have great fun dating, who find a few months' sexual comfort in one another's arms, come to the absurd conclusion that living together or even marriage would naturally increase the pleasure and amusement.

Gregory told a good story. He knew who Schopenhauer was. He had read Proust. She could discuss Thomas Mann with him. She didn't know anyone her own age who could quote from Shaw. They read Huxley together. And they laughed and made love and took long walks.

Given Anna's perilous introduction to sex, courtesy of Misha, she asked herself if taking up with Gregory was an extension of that madness. She dismissed such an idea immediately, although it was difficult to deny that the superficial similarities between the men were sufficiently outstanding to have captured her attention. Anna's misapprehensions about love were yoked to her doings with Misha. Romance, to her and no doubt millions of other young women, conjured an unfortunate mixture of charm and sexuality, the combination that had—à la Konrad Lorenz— imprinted early. Gregory's alcoholism substituted nicely for the danger of being caught kissing behind a potted houseplant. Gregory was so patently inappropriate—too old, too drunk, too selfish, too distant. He wasn't truly dangerous to life and limb, but he clearly was in a position to do damage, and that was enough to lend a familiar thrill of rebelliousness to the affair for Anna, even if she didn't know it.

The intellectual focus of their relationship was to her a welcome change from what was offered by the television-educated men of her own generation. But while Anna saw the repartee as a road in to her soul, for Gregory it was, and always had been, a way of shielding his delicate emotions from harm. Talking about Edna St. Vincent Millay poems was a warm-up to love for Anna and an evasion of love for Gregory. Of course, he pledged his deep love incessantly, but he could always retreat into his books when the going got rough, as it does in every relationship. And when the going got really rough, he drank.

THE FIRST TIME Anna saw Gregory drunk she hadn't known him long. They had gone out several times by then, chastely and respectfully. The attraction was strong but they were shy of each other. They knew something was at stake and proceeded cautiously. Anna had reviewed Gregory's play in *The Bird*, the Chicago weekly she'd worked at since college. And after her plaudits appeared in print he invited her to lunch. He drank soda water with lemon.

The courtship progressed slowly, with dinners and lunches and plays and movies. One night, after she hadn't heard from him for several days, he called her at work to invite her over for dinner.

"I'm a terrific cook," he said.

"I'm impressed," she said.

As she drove to his house she wondered if this would be the night their attraction became manifest. She arrived at the shingled cottage in a woodsy section near Evanston to find the door open. She called out his name and, hearing no reply, entered.

She found Gregory, his neck cocked against a pillow on the couch, his mouth open and contorted from the weight of his head. The rest of him lay in a heap on the hardwood floor, with one knee bent at his chest. He looked as if he had tried to get up but hadn't retained consciousness long enough to make good on the intention. It was a sultry night, and he had on only boxer shorts and one sock. It was the first time Anna had seen his body without clothes. *He has a nice body,* she thought. At forty-five, despite a little extra flesh around the middle, he still had the form of a high school athlete. His arms looked powerful. His wrists were large and his hands would still easily wrap most of the way around a football. She liked the ropey veins that wound from his biceps down along his forearms, across his wrists and over his knuckles. The muscles of his legs were bulky and well developed. You could see how they would have carried him quickly to second base after he'd swatted a dramatic, game-winning ground-rule double in the big game. His chest and arms wore a pretty pattern of fine blond hair. The hairs on each breast pointed toward the middle and there, at the sternum, it all swirled upwards and climbed to his neck. She had seen this tuft before, pouring over the open collar of his button-down shirts. And she liked the way the silky little hairs formed a narrow corridor down his belly straight into his shorts, but abruptly stopping—as if they knew what they were doing—at distinct boundaries at his ribs and waist. How do they know where to stop, those hairs? They seem to have their own convictions. Probably more than the humans they are part of. Hair will grow lushly on a head but, in most cases, not wander a millimeter below the preordained hairlines onto the forehead. How do they decide, those cells on the precipice of hairiness, not to go along with the prevailing local custom? How do they have the gall not to sprout just as their neighbors are doing? Her mind began to wander. Organs, too, have their unmistakable preferences. One's penis, for instance, likes to be crowded into close, dark, airless places, pushed and pulled through slippery emollients, tight against soft, wet, warm walls. One's head, on the other hand, does not. The genitals, the skin, the eyes, those are the organs you can see, you can recognize. So, you might feel that you know yourself intimately from years of close scrutiny in the mirror, but you wouldn't be able to recognize yourself if someone showed you yourself from the inside. That is, most of us know what a human liver looks like; you can look at pictures of them in books. But it's a rare man who knows his own liver. You really never know *your* liver, the little quirks that make it yours, the way you would know your nose from someone else's, or your fingers. You could actually walk into a room full of livers and not be able to pick yours out. Assuming you could walk into a room if your liver weren't in you.

ANNA RETURNED TO consciousness and the task of dealing with her uncomfortable reality. She felt embarrassed, as if she were betraying Gregory by staring without his permission. And she was embarrassed that she was staring rather than helping him,

although she had no idea exactly what sort of help was called
for. She was relieved to see his chest filling with breath now and
then, for at first she wondered if he were dead.

Should I help him onto the couch? she asked herself, worrying that his neck would be sore later if he remained as he was
for much longer. But she was afraid to wake him. She looked
around the room. Empty fingerprint-streaked glasses were strewn
about the floor. What had happened here? She went into the
kitchen and saw two empty scotch bottles on the table, and there
were vodka bottles in an overflowing trash pail. Dirty glasses
covered the countertop and filled the sink. Finally she understood that he was gravely drunk. Even if she were to wake him,
surely he wouldn't remember inviting her. The notion of rousing
him for his own good seemed ludicrous. And maybe he was the
violent type. Perhaps at the sight of this stranger in his house he
would reach out and slug her. So, in the semidarkness, dazed by
all the unattractive possibilities, she sat in a large chair opposite
the fallen Gregory, consulting her conscience. What to do?
Should she pile him onto the couch, drape a blanket over his
carcass, write a note and leave?

Suddenly he stirred. It took him at least a minute to arrange
himself upright. He stood shakily, his eyes half-closed. Then moving away from where Anna was sitting completely still, he shuffled
several yards toward the staircase, his bare foot making a sandy
sound as it dragged against the wood floor. He came to a stop. She
thought she could see his mental capacity just begin to function;
thought seemed to awaken him. He fumbled with his shorts—the
baggy boxers he had stripped down to in the heat—and with his
hands habitually down in front, began to urinate. Anna was mortified. And, oddly, the first image that came to mind at that moment was that of the suave, impeccably groomed Misha. This
I'm attracted to? she asked herself, staring at Gregory.

She feared breathing loudly lest he notice her and, out of anger and shame, do what? Yell? Come after her with the weapon in hand? He would fall down before he got halfway across the room. The sound of the liquid splattering on the wood was the background for the steady gong of her exaggerated heartbeat. When he finished he tucked himself in and continued toward the stairs, took two of them and, registering the impossibility of negotiating the rest, lowered himself until his hind quarters touched a step. Thus seated, he lost consciousness again.

She didn't know what to do. She was stunned, afraid to move and give away her presence. Anna could still have left without Gregory's knowing she'd been there but after a few minutes she decided she couldn't just leave him. So she tried to help him up. Gregory came to and asked what Anna was doing there. Anna explained that he had invited her, earlier that day when he had been more coherent. Then, sheepishly, Gregory asked what *he* was doing there. She helped him up the stairs. When she tucked him in he lunged for her. She unwrapped his arms from her.

"I have no intention of doing anything that only one of us would remember."

"I'll remember," Gregory said. "I think I'm falling in love with you."

"Let me know when you're sure."

"I'm sure."

"You don't know what you're saying."

"I've never been more certain of anything in my life."

"How can you know anything about someone so quickly?"

"I look at you and I know everything I need to know. You could've left me on the stairs. I know you want to stay here with me. You don't even know why yet."

"I have to go now."

When she arrived at her apartment at about one in the morning, the telephone was ringing.

"Hello?"

"I want to marry you."

Anna laughed. "Maybe you'd like to give this a little more thought?"

"*You* give it thought. I love you. Sleep well." Gregory hung up.

The next morning, before Anna went to work, Gregory called again. He sounded extremely sober.

"Hi. Listen. I'm just calling to apologize if I did anything awful last night."

"Nothing awful. Don't worry."

"I just didn't want to upset you. I can be pretty appalling when I drink. But I'm not drinking now."

"It's all right."

"Can I cook you that dinner? What are you doing tonight?"

"I don't think that's such a good idea. Why don't we just leave things as they are?"

"As they are?"

"I don't think it's such a good idea to get involved."

"You mean not see each other? Why? I'm really not drinking."

"I'm not your keeper. I don't mean to sound harsh, but you don't have to do anything for me. We hardly know each other. If that's what you like to do, I mean drinking, even just now and then, I don't think we should get involved."

"I've blown this with you, haven't I? I'm an idiot."

"You haven't blown anything. There was nothing to blow."

Gregory sounded deflated and morose. "I see. Well, you're wrong, of course. Okay, I don't want to belabor this. I can't make you see what you don't see. Take care of yourself. I'll see you."

That day at work, Anna discussed the events of the previous night with her chief advisor on the ways of the opposite sex, an editor named Dianne Qualls, her best friend at work. Dianne's down-home, South Carolina wisdom and healthy sense of indignation was a good reminder to Anna that life was often exactly what it seemed, if one only saw it clearly enough. Dianne was ten years older than Anna and with her walnut complexion, willowy frame and deep dimples, Dianne looked like someone who probably really had the experience to back up her cynical certitude on the subject of men.

"Now let me see if I understand this. You met a guy you really like. He tells you he loves you. He wants to cook you dinner. You've seen him in his shorts and you still like him. When he calls this morning to say he's crazy about you and wants to make a date, you tell him you don't ever want to see him again?"

"That's right."

"No. I must have missed something."

"Dianne, I found him comatose. I come over for our second date and he is on the floor, plastered, barely breathing. I thought he was dead. He *peed* on the floor."

"And you consider this grounds for annulment? Girlfriend, this is an unmarried heterosexual male *under* sixty-five. His IQ appears to be *above* sixty-five. So he's not housebroken. This is the late twentieth century. What do you think you're going to find out there?"

SOON AFTER THE episode at Gregory's house, Anna began dating again and found herself in the company of a bore named David at the same romantic restaurant to which Gregory had taken her.

"When you don't have to see plays, do you go to movies?" he asked her.

"I like old movies. From the thirties. Movies are so terrible now. There's no one in them you want to watch."

"I love Mickey Rourke."

"You love him?"

"You don't? A lot of women find him sexy."

"I think he's disgusting. I want to take a shower after I watch him."

David laughed at her vehemence but soldiered on.

"He's earthy."

"There's a difference between earthy and vulgar. Earthiness shows a love, an appetite for life. Vulgarity demonstrates a disrespect for it. He's vulgar."

David changed the subject hurriedly.

"It must be so great, getting paid to go to the theater. I mean, you have such a fun job."

"Waiter!" Anna called out. The waiter approached. "Another Perrier, please. David? Anything for you?"

"No, I'm fine."

When the waiter left, David persevered.

"I mean, going to plays every night."

Anna, however, was looking around the room. "Isn't that Studs Terkel?"

"Who?"

"I can't tell from here. He's a writer and a radio host."

"Oh. Don't know him. Anyway, I love going to the theater. I saw *Phantom* in New York. Bought tickets a year in advance. Made a special trip. I love Andrew Lloyd Webber. What do you think of him?"

"He has too many names."

"What do you mean?"

"Too many. Andrew Webber would be fine. Or Lloyd Webber. Even Webber Lloyd would be an improvement."

Anna fidgeted in her seat, plotting to arrange somehow for David to not want dessert. As she turned to her right, startlingly, there at the table next to her sat Gregory. The woman he sat with was a bouncy blonde who was applying lipstick while a lipstick-stained cigarette was burning in an ashtray next to her.

"Yes, Andrew Lloyd Webber is almost as bad as those country music names. Like Jerry Lee Lewis. Or Jerry Jeff Walker. I mean, using your middle name is a formality. Jerome Leland Lewis would be okay. But Jerry Lee?"

Unable to hold back, Gregory entered the discussion.

"How about Billy Butt Yeats?"

"Bobby Lou Stevenson," Anna shot back.

"Danny Gabe Rossetti," said Gregory as his date and David receded into the woodwork.

Less than two weeks later, they were together again. She was staying at Gregory's house almost every night. And they cooked and laughed and made love for several months on end.

IN THE KITCHEN Gregory was kneading dough. Anna was chopping garlic.

"I think cooking is just a substitute for sex."

"You mean all the wetness?"

He held up the wad of dough. "I mean all the fondling."

"Why is a substitute necessary?"

"Sometimes sex is inconvenient."

"Like when?"

"Like now, when my hands are oozing olive oil and you're wielding a cleaver."

"Some people might consider it an excellent time for sex."

They kissed.

"Anna, wait, I'm dripping."

"That's what we're after."

"Why don't you move in with me?"

Acknowledging that the conversation had abruptly gone serious, she put down her knife.

"I practically live here as it is."

"So why don't you give up your apartment? This place is bigger. You can have your own room to work in. The commute isn't bad."

"My apartment gives me security."

"It gives me insecurity."

"I just want to feel certain. I'm sure you don't want me staying with you just because I don't have anywhere else to go."

"I'll take what I can get. Every morning when you leave I run upstairs to see if you've taken your hair dryer with you, to see if you're planning to come back that night."

"Well, it's always nice to be invited."

"I'm inviting you. I'm inviting you for every night, for the rest of my life. We could get married."

"Do we have to decide now? Maybe we could take an apartment together, in Chicago."

Gregory smiled. "Yes, maybe."

THE APARTMENT IN Chicago had a panoramic view of the lake and downtown. A doorman was on duty twenty-four hours a day. Anna had found the sublet, a bargain. Gregory never felt entirely at ease with the luxury. He identified less with his fellow residents than with the doormen.

They had a few good years together. But little irritations—cashiers who couldn't count, the use of the word *impact* as a verb—would set off brief binges for Gregory. He always pulled himself together eventually. But then the play that had been optioned by a Broadway producer flopped, and Gregory began to drink heavily.

Anna started spending many evenings with Dianne.

"Isn't Gregory home by now?" Dianne asked after putting away the dinner dishes.

"Probably."

"This sounds serious. What's up?"

"Nothing."

"Don't give me 'nothing.' "

"He's drinking."

"Bad?"

"It's not good. He's not blitzed all the time, but it's getting to be more frequent. I don't think I can survive this." Anna started to cry.

Dianne wrapped her arms around her friend. "You want to stay here?"

"No. I have to go home. I'm just not in any hurry."

"Why do you stay with him?"

Anna sighed and thought for a moment.

"Two reasons, I guess. This is going to sound ridiculous. I have always dreaded dating because—and I gather this from all the serial daters I know—it is less about finding a person to love and to be with than about playing all those games of romance that people seem to enjoy so much. Like saying no when you mean yes—I suppose it heightens the sexual tension. But all that just seems like lying in order to secure a relationship that is ultimately supposed to be about trust. Does he like me? Will she go to bed with me? I hate all that anxiety and coyness. I think one reason I've stayed with Gregory for so long is that I am happiest when the uncertainty of the relationship is over. For most people the romance ends then. For me, it's the beginning. I hate the chase. Withholding true feelings for strategic advantage? As if you might lose something, give up part of yourself, if you say 'I love you.' Gregory says he loves me. I say I love him. Then the good part starts. No more wondering. No more maneuvering. Full of confidence, you start every day with the sole determination to demonstrate your love and bask in his. There's the romance to me—keeping it joyously alive every day when you have to face the so-called daily drudgery rather than flowers and candlelit dinners of courtship. When you're taking out the garbage. Then you can spend your life devoted to loving someone. The trouble with this is that unfortunately, even when you're with the wrong person, it's not a bad feeling. You can stay with the wrong person for a long time."

Anna was silent for a moment. Dianne said, "What's the other reason?"

"The other reason is that one of the great attractions of living with Gregory has always been that no matter how dimly I view myself, no matter how much I despise my laziness and selfishness and lack of generosity, there is always some comfort in knowing that at least I am not Gregory, a drunk who lies to himself."

Anna was a bit stunned to have heard herself say those words. "I know the whole thing is no good and no amount of love can make it better."

"That's the tragedy," Dianne said as she nodded. "Love don't conquer shit."

One night when they were in bed together, Anna finally spoke.

"We're living together like brother and sister," she began. Her aim at first was to avoid the subject of drinking. Broaching it in the past hadn't achieved good results and, frankly, she was ashamed to be living with an active alcoholic. She preferred to tell him that she wanted out for other reasons. And there were plenty of other reasons.

"You never make love to me anymore."

He felt his blood halt in his veins.

"Too much has gone wrong," she went on. "You know the

particulars as well as I. We're beyond repair. I think we should separate." He stopped breathing.

▲

The trouble with women is they think you need them, Gregory thought. She wants me to leave? Fine. Gregory sat in the room they had turned into a study. He pulled out all the drawers in the desk and began emptying them slowly, without heart, as if the tempo of the work indicated organization, a systematic mind attacking a task. But there was no system, only sadness and fury scarcely contained.

"Do the courageous thing," Gregory told Anna when she announced she wanted to end it that night. "Stay with me. I swear to god that I will do what needs to be done to keep you."

Why would she believe him? "God, how could I have blown this?" he asked himself. "I'll forever curse my stupidity if I've fucked this up with Anna. It seemed so harmless having a drink at the golf course the other day. I was parched. Spent hours in the melting sun. I was going to order a Coke but Wallace bellied up and ordered a gin and tonic and so did Lassiter and the words just knocked against my teeth to get out. Gimme a gin and tonic, I said, wishing I could take them back instantly. But I was too proud to take them back. Then I thought, Why not? I haven't had a drink in ages. Well, I hadn't had a drink in a week or so. But I was completely in control. I could take just one drink and stop. I was controlling it. And what's one little drink? Anna would never know about it. Since the play closed in New York—after a humiliating week—I haven't been thinking very clearly. Too much Valium. Ridiculous; I take the Valium to keep me calm so I won't drink out of anxiety and my brain gets so fogged that I can't find the presence of mind to say no to a gin and tonic. I'm a cocky bastard."

BUT ANNA DID notice. She always noticed.

"You've been drinking now for months," Anna said, "trying to hide it."

"I was upset. I thought you were going to leave me."

"Well, you've certainly seen to that. I *am* going to leave you."

"But you should've told me you wanted me to stop."

"It's not what I want that counts. As far as I'm concerned I didn't cause you to stop for the last five years, and if you end up on Skid Row I won't be responsible for that, either. I'm just trying to explain that if you are drinking to test me, this is a test I will fail."

"Everyone tells me, 'Do it for yourself.' Well, people quit in different ways. If it's the threat of losing the one thing, the one person you love most in life, then that's how you do it. You're my stability, Anna. I rely on you. I'm sorry. I really didn't know how you felt. I'll stop again. I'll stop for you."

Anna didn't bother hiding her exasperation anymore. After engaging in small discussions about his intermittent drinking over the last twelve weeks with no acknowledgment from Gregory that there was a problem, she was as full up with his justifications as he was with alcohol.

"Come on," she fumed. "When we first met you were sober. Three weeks later I found you dead drunk on the floor of your house. I understood finally what you were and I left. You sobered up, called me and said you were finished with drinking, and I came back. And you stayed sober for nearly five years. Did you not make a connection between our being together and your drinking habits? Look, I've said this before, but I really mean it now. I can't go on this way."

"I apologize." He whined, "I'm so sorry."

"What exactly are you sorry for? You're not sorry for getting drunk. You like getting drunk. You're sorry I'm leaving you.

I'm sorry, too. But I can't go on this way. I can't stay on out of sympathy for you. I'll turn around and find myself making the same excuses for you twenty years from now. I can't waste my life like that. Sorry."

Gregory looked at her and then his anger flared. "The drinking is just an excuse," he said at the top of his voice. "You're tired of taking chances with me. You're tired of scraping the rent money together every month. You want the romance of being with an artist but none of the reality. You've never taken a single chance all your life other than being with me. You're tired of defending me to your parents. You're ready to dump me and find a nice Jewish doctor. Yeah, dump the goy. I know what . . ."

"Gregory!" Anna heard herself shout and then took a breath. Quietly, she went on. "You seem to forget that I am in love with you. The prospect of being alone after living with you is frightening as hell. Taking chances? Being with you is the *known*, and as disturbing as life with you has been these last months, there is some comfort in your predictability. For me the courageous thing is to end it, to walk out into the unknown. The cowardly thing is to remain with an alcoholic on whom I can blame all my failures and sorrows for the rest of my life. You tell me I'm your stability? Who is mine? I have never felt more alone than I have being with you. You say you rely on me? Who am I to rely on? Part of your love for me is based on your liking the person you become when you're with me. The sober person. The personality you can't maintain without me or even, it appears, with me. I'm sure you have your reasons for falling apart at this particular moment—the play closed, writer's block, athlete's foot, a hangnail. Whatever latest offense the gods have wreaked. Idiot that I am, it's taken me this long to figure out that *this*, the guy you are right now, is the real you. The sober you is the aberration. Even in the five years you didn't drink you never really swore off drinking. You always seemed to hope that if only you stayed off the stuff for long enough that eventually you'd be able to drink again. I'm tired of wondering if you'll be conscious when I get home. Not only don't I trust you, but I hate myself for having forced you for all these years to be someone you're not."

Gregory sat at the desk facing the papers he'd accumulated over the years, remembering her words. Why dwell on the pain? He directed his attention to what he had to pack. His papers were far more orderly now than when he lived alone. Anna had imposed neatness when they moved into the apartment together. It was a nice place, made possible by the larger income she brought home after quitting the paper and taking that job, against his advice, at the ad agency. A sellout—he was living with a sellout.

"What are you going to sell?"

"Pudding."

"Pudding? Jesus. How am I going to live with someone hawking pudding?"

"Gregory, we need the money."

"I don't need the money. You need the money."

"Gregory, every time your ex comes up with some emergency that money has to come from somewhere, and it usually comes from me. It doesn't seem unreasonable to say that *we* need the money."

"Let's just go to Spain this summer. I'll apply for a sabbatical. Take a year off and we'll write. You'll finish a novel. You'll do something with yourself. We'll be happy. And we'll live there for nothing."

"I know you long to return to the glories of your youth, but this isn't going to work for right now. And I'm working on a

novel right here in Chicago. The issue isn't geography. It's paying the bills for the moment. We need this job. I wish you would
face that reality."

HE LOST THAT argument. Forget it, he ordered himself. Back to
the packing. So. Here were the successive drafts and rewrites of
the Ivan the Terrible play; the novel about an artist who is paralyzed creatively and can only paint on the days his sado-
masochistic mistress visits her bloody services upon him;
correspondence with a well-known aging actress who commis-
sioned a one-woman play about Dorothy Parker, hoping it
would help resurrect a flagging career; photographs of Gregory
and Anna; a diary and notes for future projects.

He was tossing what he was taking with him into satchels by
the side of the desk. He would be fair. "Only what's mine. I
want what's mine," he thought, throwing her papers on the
carpet. He took no care to muffle the sounds of his work. "If
she wants to rebuke my insomnia and my despair by sleeping,
let her. If she can sleep while we're breaking up, while my soul
is shattering, then it only proves how puny an intellect, how
vapid a creature she has always been. What was I doing with
her anyway? How could I have lived with her this long?" He
took another gulp from the scotch he had poured into a coffee
mug. Having drained the cup, he went into the kitchen and
fetched the bottle.

LATER, AS HE worked his way through the scotch, he thought,
Any excuse. She'd use any excuse. She doesn't even care about
sex. Maybe in the beginning she did. The sex was unbelievable
at first. I once told her I had known only one other woman
who made love the way she did, and I made *her* up. A character
in a novel. But she hasn't been interested in me for the last year.
Anyway, she knows I've been consumed by work. There's

enough guilt involved in being an artist as it is. Art is a part-time job, everyone tells you. Other things are more important than making art, they all say. Make a living, they say, then you can make art, when you have some extra time. On top of all that I need sexual insult? Lovemaking goes in cycles. One year good, a lot of sex, the next year not so much. Hey, I'm twenty years older than she. What was she expecting?

He tried to channel the anger into tidiness. There was no sound from the bedroom. He sat at the desk with only the reading lamp shining, the glare reflecting off the scotch bottle. Let her go find herself some truck driver who'll fuck her 'til he comes out the other end, that's how much my intelligence and talent mean to her, he thought. And they can grunt hello to each other for the rest of their lives, or until she gets tired of his cock, too. Or she can run into the arms of that lecher Sydney. He's dying to fuck her, if he still can. The bastard's older than I am.

Gregory put the photographs of the two of them in the pile with his manuscripts, then changed his mind. He didn't want them after all. He grabbed them and threw them back in the drawer. I don't want any pictures of her. She can have those fucking memories, he thought. I don't want them. I expunge them. I reject them. They're false. She never loved me. She couldn't possibly have loved me or she couldn't be ending it now. Yeah, she gets a story published in a big magazine and she's leaving me. She was never in love with me. She doesn't know what love is.

Then he found the letters he'd written when he was rehearsing in New York and during one of their many breakups. "Dear

Anna, The problem is I'm not the same man when I'm apart from you. This isn't a romantic lament, it's a biological fact. I've grown so dependent on you, so involved with you, so utterly at sea, completely cast adrift, rudderless, confused, frightened and thoroughly miserable when I'm without you. This separation is killing me. I don't know what to do, and I don't know how to live without you. I'm not sure you fully understand it."

He had to stop reading. He needed a drink. These letters belong to me, he thought. I get paid for my prose. They are a commodity. They might be valuable some day. If she thinks I'm leaving her some testament to my feelings for her, that she'll be able to console herself with the memory of true love after she marries some desiccated stockbroker with dollar bills where his prick should be, some jerk who wouldn't recognize passion if it were a burning spear stuck up his ass, she has another think coming.

There were forty or fifty letters. Some typed, some jotted in his tiny scrawl, pages of them written when he first went to New York for rehearsals of the play that so flamboyantly failed while she toiled in Chicago at the job he hated her taking.

He collected the letters, fastened them with a paper clip, and set them on top of the other papers he was taking with him. He would leave them out so Anna could see them, to announce his contempt to her. You want to play rough? Okay, he thought, two can play. I leave no evidence behind that I loved you.

He couldn't continue. More scotch was the only thing. He poured some and took a great swallow. He felt the alcohol kick at the nerves behind his eyes and he squinted to squeeze the sting through his system more quickly. Is that enough? Am I sufficiently anesthetized to read these letters, to make it through tonight and face the woman I want to spend my life with to-morrow morning when she tells me again that we're splitting up? No. Not quite enough for that. He tossed back another slug. He squinted again and waited, determining if that stubborn anxiety had withstood the latest salvo. *Wait, I actually feel a little better. The booze was winning.*

Anna had not slept. She heard Gregory slamming around the apartment all night. *Why had she picked now to do this? Couldn't she have waited?* She was already anxious about going to New York for her father's birthday. Her parents were sure to interrogate her about the story, and the subject of Misha would arise. She hadn't decided yet how to handle the discussion. Would she admit the account was accurate? What else could she do? Probably her distress over the story had increased her vulnerability to the Gregory problem. *If only she had kept her mouth shut until after New York. Why am I such an idiot?*

When she emerged from the bedroom showered and dressed for work that morning, she saw the scotch bottle was empty. Gregory was asleep on the floor with letters she had written to him piled on his chest. She saw the letters he had written to *her*—her property—stacked atop his manuscripts, obviously ready to be packed with his other belongings. "That jerk!" she whispered as she snatched the letters. She was enraged but immediately recognized the silliness of her anger and put them back. *How perfectly childish of him,* she thought. *I ask him to leave, he's hurt, and the punishment he comes up with is to confiscate the only materials guaranteed to make me think of him after he's gone. I guess he thinks I take some pride in having inspired him—Gregory, the great writer!—to commit his love so ornately to paper. Christ, the ego.*

She took her briefcase and tiptoed out the door, hoping to leave him sleeping and avoid another unpleasant encounter. But for the rest of the day, as she tried to work, tried to conduct meetings and talk on the telephone, she felt a constriction in her belly, a cloudy pinch in the torso that reminded her, even when she had brief moments of successful concentration, that there was some underlying reason that she was miserable. She missed him already. She imagined coming home that evening, finding him drunk, angry, accusatory, his things flung out of the closets, suitcases open on the floor, the apartment a physical manifestation of the emotional chaos within them both. And he would take days to get out. She knew him well enough to know that he would enjoy torturing her and besides, he really had no place to go. She thought about trying to live with that tension for even one day and she knew it would not be endurable. She could also imagine telling him that she had changed her mind. That she couldn't live without him, that seeing him so torn up had affected her more deeply than she expected. She *was* torn up, that was true, but just as much because she couldn't bear the way he was drawing out their pain as because she was losing her lover. She had tried to break it off so many times before and always she returned only to end the pain he inflicted on her over the breakup. The current tantrum was everything she had expected. To calm herself, she imagined an end to the tantrum. She imagined spending the next few days with him healing the rift, apologetic, tentative and uncertain, waiting for the scab to dry over a nasty wound.

EIGHT

Gregory heard the door slam. The sound reverberated in his ears like a ceiling caving in. He wasn't hungover, not just hungover. He was hungover from the alcohol he'd started drinking at the beginning of the night and drunk from what he'd had early that morning. He felt as if every muscle in his body had been ruptured. But despite the discomfort, he knew that eventually he would have to get up because he had to pee. Why were all the lights on? Oh, the lights weren't on; the sun was up, streaming in through the open blinds. Now I suppose I'll have to get up and go to school? Is that what's expected of me? I couldn't possibly teach. I'd never survive the drive.

He looked at his watch. Seven o'clock. A.M. Two hours of sleep. Okay. I'll pee. See how I feel after that. That requires standing up. He crept onto his knees, careful not to jar the jelly his brain had turned to during the night. As he stood he could feel the jelly scraping against the bony lining of his skull, which during the night seemed to have been gouged to a ragged stucco finish. He walked softly to the bathroom until he stood over the bowl and, aiming as best he could, released a painful spray of toxins.

Not the mirror, he thought, flushing the toilet. Just tooth-paste. He put his hand over his eyes and pulled the medicine-cabinet mirror open. When he peered through his fingers, there was the Valium and the deodorant rather than his damaged appearance. Why brush my teeth? Nothing could freshen the inner vapors escaping from my mouth short of decapitation. Nevertheless, he measured some toothpaste onto his index finger and rubbed the goo on his teeth and tongue. What the hell am I going to teach those bloody waifs today? I could just stand there in front of them speechless, representing a silent object lesson in the deleterious effects of alcohol on jilted lovers. What I need is a little fortification. Then I'll be fine. Then I can teach. I'll quit drinking tomorrow. I'll have another now just in sacrifice to the cause of bringing enlightenment to the heathens. They need me, those illiterates, and the only way they can have me today is drunk. If I don't have a little something I surely won't make it to school. I may not make it out of the bathroom.

Gregory slouched to the living room, his brain scraping against the stucco, looking for the scotch. He wiped his lip prints off the mug and poured scotch in, swallowed it, poured more and swallowed that. He belched. Better.

Somehow he survived the lurching twenty-minute drive to school and droned for fifty minutes about Edna St. Vincent Mil-lay to thirty-seven sleepy students. When the bell rang he headed for the caffeine. He took his styrofoam coffee cup and sat on a wall outside the cafeteria where students often sunned themselves and studied. As he sipped his coffee and thought about his stabbing head pains, a large golden retriever accompanied by no apparent owner came and sat next to him on the wall. He looked at the dog for a few moments. As he took a sip of coffee the dog nudged him. The nudge was gentle—friendly, you could say.

"Why don't blond dogs have blue eyes?" he earnestly asked his companion.

The dog did not reply.

Gregory stayed at school as long as he could, postponing the inevitable grief awaiting him at home with Anna. But when he arrived that evening, an odd thing happened. He walked in the door and she approached him so quickly that he imperceptibly backed away, thinking she was going to hit him. Then she surprised him and put her arms around him, weeping.

"I'm so sorry," she said. "Let's try again."

He embraced her with all his strength.

"Never leave me," he said sobbing.

She wouldn't until three weeks later. Gregory's drinking continued to escalate. He had chosen to read their rapprochement as an affirmation that he could behave any way he wanted without jeopardy.

Anna knew she had to get free but this time she would circumvent the discussion stage of the breakup, all that packing time, all the pauses that had allowed Gregory in the past to ooze back under her skin. This time Anna wouldn't be home for the recriminations. She would leave him a note citing all the usual reasons and her general inability to go on this way. The note explained that she packed all his things and had them delivered to his brother's in Evanston, and also that she had flown to New York a little early for her father's birthday. The message ended with a phrase that would forever puzzle the literal-minded Gregory: "I love you, but love is not enough. Anna."

NINE

Sydney was alone in his study. Sally was asleep. They had been arguing. He was dreading their divorce. It was inevitable. After four wrecked marriages (Rita gamely served as both second and third wife), he knew the signs. The five years had flown. Sally was a sultry forty-six-year-old when they met and he, her senior by fifteen years, a goatish suitor who delighted in her nearly Victorian veneer. That prim exterior only intensified his longing to peer under the shirts she buttoned at the throat. When they did become lovers her vehemence surprised him. He hadn't realized how strongly the stereotype of the woman scientist had mistakenly settled his mind about her as a sexual creature. Her jaw was firm and her face was lined, but handsomely, and, technically speaking, she looked her age. Yet she seemed a girl to him. All that science, all the hopeful, evenhanded speculation had left her so open-minded, so ingenuously hypothetical that he imagined he might have to initiate her into the intricacies of love. He had forgotten that she, too, had been married before.

Now he was contemplating their dissolution as a couple. And rather than think about the pain of it, he thought of the correspondence he had to answer. He thought of the speech he was scheduled to give at the Century Club. He thought of Anna. Why not go younger still? What's the difference between twenty years and thirty-five? Marry Anna? It would be terrible to do that to her. But she could be convinced, he believed. He knew she was attracted, and his curiosity about her, his desire for her was sometimes nearly out of his control. At times he thought his restraint preserved their friendship. He had always feared letting her down, and he couldn't have lived with her disappointment in him. Now he felt emboldened. He would risk humiliation, even outright rejection, to show her how deeply he cared. Marry her. But what kind of man would do that? She ought to have children. He'd had a vasectomy ten years ago. And even if he hadn't, he couldn't see doing that again. Not at his age. But he had grown dependent on her. He wanted her around. He loved her. Marrying him would be no bargain. But she was no more sensible than he. And I ought to be married, he thought. I need it. Marriage. To be married is to possess a live-in ally, institutional comfort, permanent reassurance; it's an exhilarating state like carnal pleasure can bring. Like music, another carnal pleasure. Just a bunch of vibrations, music is, the buzz of sexuality raised to a higher pitch. He loved organ music, which to him was like the sound of pulling magnets—what about that!—a metaphor for a metaphor for sex. We move, involuntary and giddy, to the beat of music when it is most like the rhythms of lovemaking. Irrefutable. Once you put it in, you don't want to pull it out except to immediately repeat the sublime sensation. For that brief moment, those nasty seconds when the air cools the moistened skin, the assurance that the sensation can be repeated by a simple change in direction sends the spirit soaring. In again! And the rocking becomes inexorable and mesmerizing. The senses, so acutely fulfilled, nearly numb from the hubbub, like a nose surfeited with the aromatic cacophony of too many perfumes. And she becomes a magnet, a target, a well for the thirsty, a shrine, safe harbor from the panic of that momentary withdrawal, that infinitesimal span of cessation of pleasure. She is there to save you. She accepts you, shelter from the irrational enemy, whomever you've decided that is. There is no death. In another second you'll pull it out and be able to put it in again.

It is the *not feeling* that we all want to be saved from. It is the moment away from the womb that we yearn to evade, that cold instant, that willful deprivation we endure in order to win the award of reapplication. And it is fearsome, like a midair suspension between two trapeze bars, but we risk it in order to make contact. That brief unanalyzable moment is everything we seek, the reason we yearn for recognition and acclamation. It's all just part of the flight from loneliness, the haven from *not feeling*.

The weeks I go without making contact, even living here as I do with Sally—the months of ten-hour work days, when she stays late at the lab and we hardly notice each other nude in the bathroom, the sound of her beloved Beethoven violin concerto blasting guilt at me from the living room, staining the walls with Teutonic anguish—makes me weep. Sometimes I weep when we make love during those bouts of my literary production. *Feel,* you bastard. *Feel,* the sex says to me. The sex, the music. I always used to believe that my lusts could be contained only by covering them over with a cheery wallpaper of good manners and rehearsed virtues. Women were not designed to be receptacles for my sperm, I reminded my rude, impetuous self. I would not allow myself to be attracted by appearance alone, so I made an admirable and elaborate game of learning to love a mind, a personality, a sensibility that would then be allowed to delight me down to the tip of my cock. Not a rounded breast, not the outlines of a firm behind, not the undulation of a soft hip. But, alas, try as I might to mitigate their effects with considerations that required conversation and that engaged more cerebral measurements, I could not correct my urges. How wrong I was to try. No one believes more securely in love at first sight than I do today, or at least love at first touch. You can love a skin. You can love a muscle tone. You can. And I don't mean carnal love. Nothing is more humanly moving than the feel of a baby in one's arms. No matter what my brainy theories dictate, this is not owing to the baby's understanding of Hegelian logic or its Shavian wit. You respond to the feel of the infant *because* it offers nothing but its pearly, moist skin and wet gurgles. The thought of compatibility, of getting along with this creature, never crosses your mind. The experience is purely sensual, musical, a series of vibrations reverberating against themselves, the baby's and yours, exchanged like goodwill between countries not yet enjoying formal diplomatic relations.

I can't help thinking about that church on the South Side I went to one Sunday when I was writing about gospel music. I had always had an abhorrence of chumminess with strangers, that hail-fellow nonsense, that back-clapping friendliness I never trusted when it was offered by people who would as soon embrace you as turn you in to the Gestapo. I kept to myself most of my life. My wives regretted this. I confided in few. I think it has to do with being a Jew who has a tendency to marry Christians. Keeping my own counsel, reserving my circumcised secrets. My un-Christianness, it's the part of me that wants forgiveness direct from God, not from some middleman, some sanctified gofer, some zealot too small-minded and unambitious to go off and start up his own religion so he can be boss rather than foot soldier. Why would I want to cleanse myself by confessing agonized moments to a faceless stranger? Why does telling him let me off the hook and render me good and whole again?

So in church, me the only white face, I see a man stand and, uninvited, stride to the altar where he commences to admit the wrongs he'd done his wife. In front of three hundred people.

He laments unforgivable behavior—the women, the gambling. He is eloquent. It *is* all unforgivable, horrendous, callous and selfish. But he has come for forgiveness. The forgiveness of these people will make him feel better. How extraordinary! I am not moved, I am not truly taken in by this grandstanding. To me it's as inappropriate as proposing marriage or performing some other intimate act in front of a crowd, as if the nerviness proves the depth of the sincerity. He is pretending to care about what these other people in the room think, what I think. I am not fooled for a minute; I don't forgive him. But, miraculously, the majority rules. The congregation shouts its approval. Forgiveness is his. Then, his soul purified, his diaphragm empty of speech, the channels of evil flushed, he steps down, walks toward the congregation members, and begins to shake each person's hand. They rise one by one as the sinner approaches, the handshakes growing more vigorous. Some reach out to hold him by the shoulders, several embrace him outright, and suddenly I am in awe. I envy the fellow. He is making people feel. And for that alone they love him. It's real love. I wish so hard that it came as naturally to me that I am sobbing. The handshake that started out as a superficial gesture takes on a life of its own. Sartre was wrong. *Heaven* is other people.

There was something sumptuous, sensual and frighteningly abandoned about the love in that room, and at the same time innocent. How much easier to find it en masse than in one other person. One other criticizing, scrutinizing person. How much less terrifying is this public fix than the kind of one-on-one microscopic examination we subject our spouses to and our children and friends. All right, it's not five years' worth of love, not a short marriage's worth, but it's a start. I've been alone all my life. And it shows.

God. Three o'clock. Enough. I will climb into bed now, press my hairy belly against Sally's curled back, absorb her warmth and cover her with mine. I'll pass my hand over her majestic rump until it awakens, even as the rest of her sleeps. And then, if she's not too angry with me, even if she already knows that she is leaving soon, she will respond like the fellow who's taken too much whisky for his thirst, automatically, drunkenly. She will move against me, not out of lust, not out of a desire to turn the throb between her legs into a spark of completion, but to make contact. We will always want this simple thing, after the desire is gone, after habitual, routine anger has ossified the suppleness of our affection. After the divorce. If not with each other, then with someone else.

TEN

Sydney had mentioned that Sally would be out of town attending a scientific conference. Anna had run out on Gregory, finally leaving what she hoped was a nonnegotiable-sounding note. She also hoped that he would believe she'd gone to New York early, obediently follow the clothing and books she'd sent to his brother's place and settle there temporarily without fuss or argument. Of course, he would probably keep calling and even try to visit. She planned to change the locks. She only had a few days of vulnerability before she left for New York. As long as she didn't have to face him again, debate again her right to break it off with him.

When she arrived, Sydney made her coffee. Then they sat on the sofa together, not two feet apart, as she laid out for him the details of the last few months with Gregory. Sydney was eager to hear it all.

"I didn't know about the drinking," he said.

"It was too embarrassing to talk about."

"Well, I'm glad we're talking now. Friends can say embarrassing things to each other."

"Yes, you're a good friend. I can talk to you." But then, as if to give the lie to her avowal, she was silent for quite a while.

Finally she spoke. "You know, Gregory was pretty jealous of you. Always asking about our lunches."

"What did he ask?"

"He would wonder aloud, coyly, what a famous author like you would want with someone like me. Fundamentally it was kind of flattering, it was out of jealousy. But superficially, the way he expressed it was kind of insulting. I think he probably wanted to come along. He thought, I'm sure, that he, being a writer, would be much better, more stimulating, company for you. Given that, he probably assumed that there was something between us. You never liked him, I gather. You've probably been sitting around waiting for us to break up."

Sydney put his glasses on to peer at Anna. The gesture was solely for effect; they were his reading glasses. He was counting on using the extra time between her question and his anticipated response to deflect the issue entirely. Upsetting the rhythm of conversation would spoil his interrogator's concentration, he hoped. Her question was put accusingly, he thought, implying Sydney had seamy motives for wanting Gregory out of the picture. A few speech-free moments would dilute the intensity of her insinuation. If he waited long enough to answer she might drop the whole thing. Certainly he wanted Gregory out of Anna's life. Even when Sydney first married Sally, an affair with Anna while Gregory was still a factor would have meant cheating on two partners rather than a more manageable one. The fewer the complications the better, in all cases.

"I take that as a yes," Anna said. Sydney was sitting quite close to Anna now, his upper body leaning in toward her. Oh boy, I'm out of one frying pan and right into the fire here, she thought. I've been so dumb. He is steering us into romance. Get her to talk about her love life and how it failed and use the opportunity to advertise your own assets as a lover. That old strategy. Can I do this again? Can I choose so wrongly again?

Can I fly in the face of good sense? Yes, Sydney has his virtues. He doesn't drink. That's a big plus right now. He's younger than Misha. Barely. Well, it's a step in the right direction anyway. Maybe when you're as sick as I am, wellness is achieved in small increments. By the time I'm sixty-two, I will be dating someone age-appropriate for a woman in her thirties. Sydney actually has a lot going for him. He's been a good friend for years. I trust him. He's selfish, but in a way that isn't too obnoxious. And he is good at avoiding situations that disturb him. That means he's comfortable with himself most of the time, which means I'm comfortable when I'm with him. And he's known me too long to be looking for a mere fling. No, he wants it all. And for the rest of his days. What about the rest of my days? What do I do after you're gone? Or, worse yet, while you're lingering? And what about children, Sydney? You couldn't possibly want to have more children, squalling babies, sleepless nights. She looked at his thin arms and imagined them rocking a screaming infant. It would be an injustice to subject him to it. Anyway, he's told me more than once about his vasectomy.

But he's clever. He's grilling me, all these sideways interrogations about my past romantic failures, hoping to awaken an interest in him. I do love him, but it's unfair to do this to me. Did I love Gregory? he wants to know. If he means did our souls interlink, the answer is no. It wasn't that kind of high-grade love. Maybe for a little while our borders overlapped. No, it was bargain-basement love. Love that's been marked down, stamped "irregular." I now understand I mistakenly believed that love is inextricably linked to pain. I accepted that tenet because I loved Gregory and I got pain in return. Suffering a great deal of pain in connection with loving Gregory just seemed part of the arrangement and I didn't question it. It was like a job, loving Gregory. Gregory provided employment for me. I was there to rescue him from himself, and I admit I enjoyed every minute of it for about four years. Then the drinking began again and I would have preferred to call 911 during his emergencies. Let the professionals handle this new "crisis." A manuscript would be rejected. A grant would fall through. An ex-wife needed money. A cold was coming on. There were solid weeks when the sound of the telephone would trigger a Pavlovian panic in him. More bad news, he was sure. I don't know about love. I have no longing for him. I don't yearn. But I feel responsible. I wish that would go away. Fortunately, the other bad feelings I lived with for years miraculously disappeared when I made up my mind today that this was the end. I only hope this freedom from anxiety lasts. Every day, for years, I wondered if he would be drunk, sprawled on the floor when I came home. Who needs the angst? Frankly, the pleasures I had with Gregory, I have simply written them off. I will do without them. I will be lonely. But I have to remind myself that I was lonely with him. I just didn't notice it because he was there. The noise fooled me.

"Anyway, what I feel for you is quite different," Anna said. "I sometimes think my feelings for you are real the way they aren't with anyone else. That's why the friendship has been so good for so long. I envy you having Sally. I know you were no angel before you met her. But you made a real effort to change in order to make her happy. You worked a little less, I think. You told me your previous wives felt as if they weren't a part of your life. You seemed to try to spend more time with Sally. I envy her for that. I've actually promised myself not to talk to you about Sally. There's something in a good marriage that shouldn't be shared with outsiders. Even a close outsider. And I didn't want to transgress that line, even though it meant leaving a blank in our friendship. As it is, my friendship with you is my one untainted association. I love you very much."

Sydney was moved beyond words. He could hear his heart pumping more strenuously at the news. "Yes, I love you, too."

They sat in silence as they listened to the voices in their heads repeating what they had just heard themselves utter.

A fire was burning in the fireplace. Sydney's arm was draped over the back of the couch. If he merely dropped it down it would graze Anna's cheek. Am I preparing for a seduction? He had asked himself the question even as he artfully piled the kindling before Anna's arrival. He was still asking. He thought it a breach of trust to attempt to compel Anna to do something about which she had any compunction. In seduction there is always the element, no matter how small, of unfriendly persuasion, a notion that the seducer must convince his victim to couple against better judgment. Sometimes, in Sydney's experience, when rationalizations against making love look good on paper but in the face of an embrace seem feeble, all it takes is the chance to prove the meaningfulness of a kiss. One must slyly arrange for that powerful moment when your eyes lock and you both know that only a kiss can follow. At that moment there are still crucial seconds during which the hesitant partner can halt the action and argue against consummation. The trick is to slip silently past that juncture. And the only way to do that, Sydney knew, is to slow the action, ease into gear. The slowness of the descent onto Anna's mouth would be too delicious to hurry. He wanted to take those few seconds to savor her scent, gauge the bodily fluids evaporating from her pores, register against the skin of his mouth her temperature intensifying as he moved nearer. He wanted to retain a vision of her surrendering expression, blurring as he moved in. He wanted to see her part her lips to welcome his entry, to feel her breath before he tasted it. They sat on the couch saying nothing, fatigued from all the talk. He put his arm around her and leaned her head back against his shoulder. He kissed the top of her head and then pulled away to look at her form, which was licked by the reflective light of the fire. She turned to see why he had moved, as he knew she would, and he caught her gaze. Don't ruin this, he thought. He wanted her so much that he needed to prolong the glory of anticipation. His erection was jumping in his lap. He needed to feel her skin, cover her with a layer of his affection. He put his hand to her cheek and she drew him to her, looking in his eyes all the while until he was too close to look anymore.

ELEVEN

After, Sydney wanted to talk about the future. He wanted there to be a future.

"Were you planning this for a long time?" she asked.

"About seven years."

They lay in silence, both smiling.

"I suppose I owe Gregory a debt," Sydney said.

"What do you mean?"

"Well, if he hadn't behaved so badly we wouldn't be here now. Like this."

"No, I suppose not."

"On the other hand, if it weren't for him I could have saved myself a marriage."

"What do you mean?"

"I wouldn't have married Sally."

"Are you serious?"

"Not if I could have married you."

"That's what you wanted to do?"

Now I take the plunge, he thought. "Yes. That's what I would like to do now. But if you're opposed I won't press. I realize that I have far more to gain than you. I am willing to take you on any terms."

Anna, still reeling from having slept with Sydney, was now stunned by Sydney's suggestion. Getting proposed to, as a rule, put Anna on edge. Gregory's constant proposals were a strain on her. She hated saying no to him, but couldn't imagine saying yes. The thought of marriage to Gregory was always jarring, slightly insulting, as if she were being offered a bad deal dressed up as a good one. The only good marriage she knew was her parents', and she couldn't see that for herself. She couldn't see sacrificing her life for any man. And, surprisingly, given that Anna didn't date much, these proposals seemed to pop up with alarming frequency. Anyone she'd ever seen for more than a month had proposed. One after another, men would lay the offer on the table as if it were the ultimate sacrifice. Grim-faced, they proposed, doing the one thing they most didn't want to do, but were willing to do for *you* because, you see, they loved you so deeply. You, who they assumed desired nothing more intensely than marriage. You, who were waiting hopefully for matrimony, were expected to leap into their solemn, sacrificing arms. A somberness bathes the announcement; a certainty, too, that it will be accepted with impolite glee. He wants me to make him miserable? Anna thought when Gregory proposed. Not on your life.

"What about Sally?"

"We're getting divorced. She's going to New York until we sort things out."

"What?"

"We're getting divorced. We've been to lawyers."

"When did this happen?"

"It's been long in the making. We've known for a while."

"You never said anything about a divorce."

"You were all caught up in Gregory troubles. And I, selfishly, didn't want to spoil the possibility of this with you."

"So you want immediately to get married again because you believe so fervently in the soundness of marriage, having tried it five times?"

Sydney sighed.

"Yes. Plus I love you."

This threw her "affair" with Sydney under a new light. There had always been something faintly taboo about their friendship, yet because it was nonsexual, their public appearances were fun to flaunt. No one would believe it, but they were only friends. And everyone's certitude that Sydney was making adulterous hay charged their encounters with the electricity of possibility.

"I want to have children."

"Yes, I know. Well, of course, the vasectomy could be reversed. But I have three kids. Do I want any more? I never thought I'd have more. But then I never thought I'd be in love this way again. I don't know. We have to talk about kids. Your life changes so much when you have kids. The sounds in the house. The smells. Lovemaking changes."

"I thought you were looking to change your life."

"Yes." He laughed. "You're a pretty big change all by yourself."

SYDNEY AWOKE AT five and sat up, looking at her body. He couldn't believe his luck. The view of her seamless form there on his bed arranged before him to assimilate and idolize was almost more than he could stand without it triggering a tremor of physiological anguish and reverence, a small personal earthquake within. His passion that night sometimes seemed so fierce that he feared he might harm her in his frenzy. He would have to watch himself in future. A caress might get away from him, all because her tongue tipped a certain way, or a low moan escaped from some hidden place in her. She had movements and habits and arches in her back that could turn his tender embraces

Barbara Shulgasser-Parker

into rib-cracking clutches. Holding back would be nearly impossible. He wanted to take her in utterly, compress her into a thing he could carry with him always, condense and contract her with the force of his body, with the press of a kiss, with the thrust of his hips. And in that yearning there was a part of him that wanted to be transported all the way, as far as the hankering would take him, to teach him what it might be to lose control completely. He feared hurting her yet he felt constricted by the dishonesty in suppressing his obsession. Of course, there was no choice. It would be absurd to crush the life out of the object of his love just for the sheer love of her. So delicate, the body's integrity, always at such risk of injury. Instinctively we understand its defenselessness, that it is frangible, penetrable. So even at the moment of release Sydney held back. How little it takes to end a life. People die of lesser violence than ordinary sex. Think how small a violation is a bullet hole, delivered in a quick smack. No foreplay, no lead-up, just a loud report and the sound of slumping flesh. Death by intercourse would be much more laborious. There must be some weird, demented sexual pleasure in being a torturer, applying oneself to pain-inflicting bodily invasion, Sydney thought. The grubby, hands-on devotion to slow destruction. Imagine how efficient, by comparison, the bullet. Just thirty-eight millimeters. A hole so small can finish you off. A man isn't much better than a balloon when it comes to standing up to punctures in his hide. How little it takes to disrupt the system, the coherency, the pressure holding the insides in and the outside out. Funny that we insist on perceiving the *gun* as the instrument of danger. It *looks* menacing. You can point it. It has weight and heft. But it's the bullet, that sleek little plug, that does you in. The same with a knife, slender, cold, thin. The thing slips in, hardly disturbing a profile, but by separating the cells that hold you together, by interrupting the interior channels and corridors, it's all over. Just a simple, economical slit. Am I, he mused, making the case for the slam-bam-thank you-ma'am school of sex? It would probably be much safer. No wonder feminists call me a misogynist, he laughed to himself.

Would she marry him? he wondered. She'll go to New York to see her parents and the vividness of this moment will fade. "Please God, don't let me lose her to good sense." Then he berated himself. If nothing else happens, this will have been enough. He looked down at Anna's shoulder rising with each breath, her torso articulated by bands of bones, like the spokes of an umbrella moving against an inner wind. What luck, he thought. What luck.

GOD GAVE
US APPETITES

TWELVE

With her swollen feet throbbing and a pain shooting through her lower back, Sonia stood sinking in the mud, surveying the site of her future quarters. She and Max had moved thirty-seven times from the time of the liberation of the Kovno ghetto in 1944 to this day in 1954. Through Lithuania, Poland, Czechoslovakia, Russia, Germany and France. She had been so happy in Paris. Why couldn't they have stayed there? But no, we had to come to New York to be near some distant relatives we'd never met. And then it was walkups in the West Nineties, and worse yet, the Bronx. Finally things got better and we went to the garden apartment in Queens. Then the lavish apartment on Central Park West. A view of the park. Doormen. What service.

She muttered a curse at Max and this, the latest of his schemes. Building a house in Scarsdale. Where they don't even want Jews. She looked across a wretched landscape, a parcel where great old trees had been cleared to make way for their house. I am a cosmopolitan woman, she thought, pulling down on the gabardine maternity dress that had become too tight around her broadening girth. What am I doing moving to the country?

The workmen were laying a foundation in the middle of the two acres for which Max had ingeniously negotiated, even if he did say so himself. "With children you can't stay in an apartment," Max had said. "New York City is no place for children."

And what about a place for *me*? Sonia thought. Do you think the children are going to live here alone? Yes, for *you* it's ideal. You will go into town every day and, exhausted by the gray corridors of concrete, return to this haven of trees and tranquillity. I'll give you tranquillity. You'll come home to trees and I'll be swinging from them. No doorman, no one to carry the groceries in, park the car, fix the drain when it clogs.

Sonia could hardly bear the thought of the isolation. She looked at her ankles, which were aching. Were there still beautiful shapely bones under the pillow of swelling? Would she ever see them again? She looked up at the field where the house would soon rise and tears began to fall.

"You have to have a home," Max told her. "You've been wandering since you were thirteen-years-old, parents killed, house stolen away, moving from one place to another, first a closet, then a one-room, one rental after another. You can't carry this impermanence around with you forever. You have to trust *some*thing," Max pleaded. "We need a home, something that's ours. It's the only way to wash our hands of the past. You'll see, it will be a change of luck for us, this house. You'll see."

"Hi, Dad."

"Anyushka, hi."

"Are you in the middle of something?"

"I'm never in the middle of something when I hear from you. Things instantly come to an end when you call."

"I'm not sure if I should regard that as a good thing or a bad thing."

"Well, you'll have to agree that all things must come to an end. Therefore things coming to an end must be a natural good. If your call ends them faster it's practically a mitzvah. It's always a good thing when you call."

"Well, I really have nothing important to report. Just calling to say hi, so if you're busy I'll let you go."

"I'm not busy. Just finishing a relatively silly piece for *Commentary*, that thing about why Jews hate their mothers."

"Do Jews hate their mothers?"

"Everybody hates their mothers. I'm just targeting a select audience. Hating your parents is one of the job requirements of a healthy child."

"I must not be very healthy. I don't hate my mother. And I don't hate you."

"Yes, that's the tragedy. We worked so hard on you and look how you disappoint us." Her father laughed, but he didn't hear Anna laugh along.

"Hello?" he said, still laughing. "Are you there?"

Anna replied, "*Do* I disappoint you?"

"Oh, terribly. Your mother and I cry about how ashamed we are. Our daughter, she's so bright and pretty. She writes beautifully. And we're not the only ones who think so—big magazines pay her for her work. She calls. She visits. Where did we go wrong? We constantly wonder."

Another silence followed.

"Hello? Anna?"

"I never know when you're kidding," she said.

"I'm not kidding. You're my pride and joy, Anyushka. Don't you know that? Oh, there's the other phone. The secretary isn't here. I'll see you soon, yes?"

"I love you, Dad."
"Bye."

WHEN ANNA WAS a girl she knew her father the way a daughter can know. She knew parts of his biography. The date of his birth. All the dates—the one on the Jewish calendar, which was the first night of Passover; the one on his passport, which shaved six years off his actual age because the man who had forged the passports that would enable Max and Sonia to leave Lithuania during the war was in a rush and used one all-purpose date on about a dozen documents; and the one that Social Security had assigned him thirty-five years after he had become a citizen, when he petitioned to correct his records so he could collect what America owed him at age sixty-five.

Anna also knew what he liked to eat and what made him laugh and what books he read. When she was a child she would sit at the end of the couch and learn the title and authors of great books by staring at the dust jackets resting on his stomach as he read. They were a family of worldly Jews. That was the legacy Max was passing on. Max was the first in this line. *He* had been raised in an Orthodox home and, to the shame of observant relatives, ignored the prescribed rituals to become a religious renegade. The family would have been distressed enough had he simply abjured devoutness. But he was a nose-thumber. To his renouncement of the religious life he merrily added sacrilege, pouring his vigorous skepticism into popular books, magazine articles and television appearances characterized by his exotic but lucid English. The exposure won him renown and remuneration, sufficient to support his unseemly—in the eyes of the more religious relatives—acquisitiveness. That was the last laugh—making a living out of tweaking the pious. He relished willfully stirring up an already bitter dish with his loud and public denunciations of Old World religiosity. Although he enjoyed the philosophical arguments that were the foundation of Judaism, he had no patience for the dogma or for the blind faith. Where, after all, had God been when the six million perished? Anyway, he liked *dis*agreement, not acquiescence. Harmonious, mass acceptance on faith was the solid foundation, he would say, of Nazism. Get more than three people patting each other on the back and it doesn't take long before they're lynching blacks and gassing Jews. Max's moral duty, he said, was to dismantle such dangerous doctrine by scrutinizing the rules and regulations of Judaism, and other religions, for the fundamental flaws. He saw himself as a sort of civil servant, like a building inspector protecting the public from unsound philosophical structures. And he meant to perform his duties in public, out loud, so everyone could hear. "God gave us appetites not to tempt us but to awaken us to our glorious polymorphous senses," he would say. "It is the understanding and embracing of the appetites all men have in common that will lead us to brotherhood."

He once told a television interviewer, "The time when each of us feels most indubitably like himself, when each of us appears to be experiencing the pinnacle of individualistic sensation—I'm talking about orgasm—that's the time we are, in fact, most like everyone else. How different from mine do you really think is going to be your orgasm? Statistically speaking—in terms of intensity and duration and hormonal output—the differences will be negligible. I think it tells you something about where we stand in the universe that when we believe ourselves to be most unique, that is when we are most ordinary and interchangeable. Eh?"

Religion, he argued, curbed the fulfillment of wants. Religion judged pleasure evil and scolded its seekers. The strictures against foods, sex and other joys set us to killing and pillaging in the name of want and covetousness, he would explain. So why eat kosher? What kind of lovers of the word would prohibit writing on the Sabbath? Would God really take offense at the man riding in a car on his day of rest? Isn't it more restful to ride than walk? And if God is so petty to worry about matters of such insignificance, why should we worship him or her?

What he loved about Judaism was its combination of the spiritual and intellectual rigor. "Contrary to popular opinion," he liked to say, "the Bible is not a book about God. Its prime objective is to talk about man." Then he would recount the story of Rabbi Hillel, who was interrupted in his study by a gentile. "Legend tells us that Rabbi Hillel was asked by a gentile if he could teach him the Bible in a hurry. Rather than explain that such an undertaking would be impossible, even absurd, Hillel simply told him, 'Love thy neighbor.' And that is the primary message of the Bible. Man interacting with man. Everything else is history and commentary."

In fact, in keeping with Max's belief that Judaism was primarily about man's relation to man rather than to God, it had become a family tradition on Yom Kippur for Anna, Max and Sonia to ask for the others' forgiveness. God would only write in the Book of Life those who had asked forgiveness for their transgressions from the people they transgressed. And, as Max liked to say, God also looked kindly upon those who were willing to forgive.

"Dad, I'm sorry if I did anything that hurt you this year. I hope you can forgive me," Anna would say. Max's usual reply was, "I can't think of anything, but if there *was* something, I forgive you," and he would give her a kiss on the forehead to seal the transaction.

"When the Bible was written," Max would go on, "people had all kinds of holy stuff. Holy statues, holy robes, holy places. But for the first time, the Bible proffered a new and overriding concept: holy *time*. In the first chapter of Genesis where the Almighty created practically everything, don't you think it would have been logical for him to throw in some holy real estate? Fence off a nice prime section of the Garden of Eden and designate it holy? Pious Jews could celebrate bar mitzvahs there and hold membership drives and solicit ads for their journals. Mind you, He planted his most precious possessions there—the Tree of Life and the Tree of Knowledge—but there is no mention anywhere that he anointed the place as holy. What he did do, in a chapter further along, was something much more clever. He took the seventh day—a day!—and he called *that* holy. What is a 'day?' A day is a length of time. He sanctified a specific bit of time. And since then, we believe in the sanctity of time. Of course, we have our religious rituals whereby we sanctify the wine and bless the challah, but the wine we drink and the bread we eat. The day we cannot consume. It passes each week and then it returns, sanctified yet again. The greatness of Judaism, and Christianity, too, in this sense, is that of all worldly things and possessions, we value the most a thing for which we don't even have a definition. What, after all, is time? Unless you're Einstein and can calculate a mathematical formula, who can say what is time? So, in the end, we believe that it is more important to be than to have. To believe in our hearts rather than to hold in our hands.

"A great example of this is our belief in the ten commandments. Moses received the stone tablets on which the commandments were written directly from God. Those tablets, they were an artifact, a museum piece! Yet Moses broke the tablets deliberately.

"Jews believe that the ideas on the tablets are holy but not

107

the tablets themselves, which were made of stone, stone no different and no holier than any other stone. As a matter of fact, some say that Moses's greatest deed was the breaking of the tablets.

"He realized it was the message, not the medium. But his people were not ready for the message so he didn't hesitate to destroy the artifact and let time, yes, time, prepare his people. He, Moses, a mortal, could not conquer time, but he tried to do the best a mortal could do, and that was to attempt to master time. The Bible, essentially, teaches man how to master time."

We value time and not things. You'd think Max would thus observe the Sabbath. But no. He did, however, demonstrate in his love of life a profound awareness that it was short. He enjoyed himself.

He knew so many ways to enjoy himself. He enjoyed good wine and food. He loved good books. And he loved beautiful clothes. The staples of his wardrobe—the ascot, the silk vest, the custom-made shirt—were possessions he valued, Anna knew, but it was also clear that if they were taken away, his mood would not suffer. He had lived without. He had certainly done without. But given the choice, naturally, he preferred the momentary morale boost provided by sliding his arms into the cool sleeves of a custom-made silk chemise. He enjoyed being cosseted in the comforting drape of a linen suit that had been measured and cut specifically to his form. He liked to leave undone one of the four buttons on the right cuff of his jacket sleeve, soliciting comment whenever he signed an autograph or the bill in a restaurant.

Her father's wardrobe spoke to Anna of self-confidence, a subdued peacockishness that didn't get in the way of decency and humanity. Max dressed to prove that you can care about the morality of mankind and look good, too. So, for many years Anna unconsciously mimicked her father's style of dress. As a child she would explore her father's cedar-infused closet with its neat row of hanging suits, all of them simple, dignified and elegant. Her mother dressed beautifully, too, but women's clothes always seemed to Anna unnecessarily complicated. There were so many nonnegotiable requirements. To look really good in women's clothes it was crucial to have breasts, and not just any breasts, but breasts of a certain shape and size, affixed at a certain angle to the correct quadrant of the rib cage. You had to have hips, not too wide and not too scrawny. You needed legs of some distinction. Ankles were a must. Anna worried that she had been shortchanged in the bosom department, and women's fashion was unforgiving on this count. Men's clothing seemed designed to allow any fellow, no matter what pathetic shape, to appear to be relatively broad-shouldered, narrow-hipped, stream-lined and sharp. Men were offered more forgiveness for their flaws. Wrinkles added character to a man's face and the stigma of mortality to a woman's. To Anna, women's clothes always seemed so constricting. Men complain of tight collars and suffocating ties, but at least, she thought, they could run for a bus without worrying that a sharp wind might expose their genitals. No, men's clothes were fairer, more egalitarian. And for Anna, Max's closet was an exemplar of the theory. All those suits of nondescript color hanging with soldierly discipline. The fabrics were all constructed, like an Impressionist's painting, of tiny flecks of faint hues. A gray suit was not just a gray suit but a tableau of multicolored pebbles—granite, pewter, silver, slate, blue, black and graphite. And those suits looked so well on Max. The gray ones echoed the metallic gray of his wavy hair, and all of them gave him the powerful shoulders that nature hadn't, even though the man obviously required such shoulders to bolster a neck strong enough to hold up that lively, full-of-brains head. By the time she was thirty, Anna discovered that she no longer owned a skirt.

Max's breezy writings and informal manner won him admirers and friends in the gentile world, associations to which the family also objected. "These people find you an object of ridicule," one of the few cousins still speaking to him liked to say. "Your so-called fans accuse you behind your back," he said. "They look at you and think 'Christ killer.' "

True enough. There was a faintly derogatory aspect to the respect awarded Max. He wasn't revered, he wasn't held as a secular saint, like Elie Wiesel, whom Max liked to refer to as the "professional Holocaust survivor," owing to his fervent campaigning to win the Nobel Prize. No matter how well the various media seemed to love Max, he was to them a kind of circus act, the amusing Jew with the cute accent who spoke in catchy sound bites. Everyone recognized that what Max did he did well, but how much better it would have been not to need such a thing as a smart Jew who gleefully and logically cut down everyone's belief systems with funny one-liners. To him Jesus Christ was "a nice Jewish boy." Some people, understandably, objected to his views.

Max was quick, earthy and urbane, a combination that made him attractive on talk shows and at lecterns. He was a pen for hire; glib, sarcastic, serious, just the man to speak, write or think unconventionally about religion, to comment when biblical artifacts were dug up, to explain the historical meaning of a holiday or to clarify the conflict between warring factions at odds anywhere from Borough Park to Jerusalem for newsmen who needed pithy quotes. Television was especially suited to his gifts. Max, who could successfully have defended fascism in debate, had a grave respect for the necessity of shallowness, and television made him glow with easy-to-fathom wisdom as if he were born to the cathode ray. His philosophical monographs ran deep but, where the electronic media were concerned, he knew that style—a phenomenon of which he was a careful student—was more than a match for substance.

He reserved the substance for his academic career. He occupied an endowed chair at Columbia in comparative religion, and from that lofty post broadened his field of attack to include Christianity, Buddhism and Islam. His appetite for criticism was huge, like all his appetites.

Although professionally he lived a life of the mind, the worldly beckoned and he responded eagerly. He would never pass up a game of seven-card stud. A bottle of vodka called to him. But of all his weaknesses, his greatest weakness was for beauty. That weakness was most evident in his tenderness toward Sonia. Max, already narrow and light-footed, seemed to lighten even more in Sonia's presence. To say he worshiped her would imply his sentiments were rooted in choice. In fact, he was unreasonable and illogical in his susceptibility to her. Anna, versed in the skills of family diplomacy, knew Sonia's appeal could soften Max's disciplinary vigor whenever he denied Anna some fancy. Anna orchestrated her mother's intervention over many a contested paternal directive.

Sonia was born in Poland, a fact that on its own Max treated as if it were the punchline to a hilarious joke. According to him, no one so beautiful could be from such a negligible country—a piece of breakaway Lithuania, as his nationalistic history teachers instructed him when he was a schoolboy. The concept of Polish beauty, he would remark—nearly incoherent with laughter—was an oxymoron flagrant enough to send him into what seemed to the young Anna life-threatening spasms of giddy breathlessness. Sonia would smile. Her tolerance, Anna knew, was proof of her devotion to him.

Sonia was the center of his life. In letters to Anna, written when her parents were traveling, Sonia and family were always his focus, and so was amusing them.

"We got to Palm Springs," he wrote her one winter when she was at college, "*sans bagage*. The luggage was directed to Los Angeles, where I hope it will have a very good time. Furthermore, for some mysterious reason, our reservations at the spa were canceled by a person and/or persons unknown. Also not arriving with us was the balmy weather normally reigning in this part of the world. We expected eighty degrees. We only got about thirty-two-and-a-half of them. Fortunately, your mother has a coat perfect for this temperature range. It's just too bad that this particular garment happens to be in New York.

"Some people have all the luck. They wake up in the morning and, boom, they're in trouble, just like that. I have to travel three thousand miles and spend thousands of dollars."

Sonia was not from an Orthodox background, and Anna understood that her parents' union was viewed as an unsuitable marriage by all the relatives. During holidays celebrated under Max's orders in sharply abridged versions ("for the tradition, not the religion," he would say), Sonia would ask him to remind her what special ceremonies and foods were required for the given occasion. Do we dip apples in honey at Passover? Rosh Hashanah? Purim? Which is the one where we wash the hands all the time?

ANNA HAD BEEN sent for religious instruction where she learned the answers to these questions, and when she needed help with Hebrew school homework she turned to her father. From her mother she learned other lessons necessary to the good life. Sonia loved to dance and taught Anna all the crucial elements of the expert hip-shaking, shoulder-dipping, toe-bending and arm-waving in her repertoire. Anna, more athletic than poised, mimicked her mother's fluid steps as best she could, but she scarcely matched Sonia's grace. When Anna and Sonia practiced the rumba to Harry Belafonte records, even Max, with his two left feet, would come to watch the pair whirl around the living room and tap his feet to the rhythm. His girls would laugh and scream and perspire in the effort. And as he remembered times that seemed impossible to even imagine, he would smile.

"I'm calling the talent scouts," Max would cry. "You two belong on television. Does Nureyev need a cha-cha partner?"

Families are the grand contradiction in every person's life. If you are lucky, you grow up under the supervision of a benevolent parent or two, and perhaps, again, with luck, a benign sibling who isn't psychotic, violent or prone to jealous rages. And you live that way for perhaps sixteen to eighteen years with these people. By the time you are sixteen and able to dress and feed yourself and make an occasional sound decision, you find yourself still in the close company of people who knew you before you were capable of performing these elementary personal tasks. Here you are, feeling pretty good about the dressing and feeding and deciding, so good and so confident that it looks to you as if the people who taught you to do these things, who have been doing them far longer than you, are imbeciles who are damn lucky they've made it this far, just in time for you to begin correcting their errors. And then, many years later, you realize that the way you know your dearest friends, your spouse, the people who work with you—all the people you have collected since rationality and toilet-training were under your belt—-that you will never know your parents that way, that well. This is because when you met them you were unable to process the information that being in their company could provide. You were too busy spitting up and shitting yourself. And by the time you've met your parents, people who, from your point of view, seem inordinately consumed with matters of your well-being, they've already lived a good portion of their lives during which the thought of you, specifically, never occurred to them. No wonder so many people in their forties end up in therapist's offices trying to figure out who they are and, by extrapolation, who their parents were. Now, on the subject of parents, women who habitually take up with older men obviously have some kind of father problem. What was Anna's problem? She often asked herself that question and, unable to formulate a satisfying answer, feared that she was doomed to forever repeat her romantic errors.

She was sure only of one thing. She had always craved her father's approval. This was indeed a problem. Although her father adored her, he thought so highly of her as a human being that it seemed absurd to him to need to tell her how extraordinary he thought she was. So he didn't. And so she never knew of his admiration except through occasional references her mother might casually make of her father's pride. The withheld praise came not out of meanness but of the natural presumption a highly self-confident person like Max would make, that Anna, too, thought enough of herself to need no further encouragement from others. Max actually admired what he thought was her independence; an aloofness she developed to compensate for the craved but rarely received praise. He read it as defiance and self-confidence. So did most people.

Once, when she was in high school, she brought home a paper she'd written to show off the A emblazoned in red at the top of the first page. Max read it and, taking her work as seriously as he would one of his graduate student's, he criticized the writing and thinking rigorously. Even though she had earned an

A from her teacher, he asked her to rewrite it as he'd advised, just for the exercise. She grudgingly complied.

Anna was not an obviously rebellious teenager. Marijuana hurt her throat. Alcohol put her to sleep. Owing to Misha's influence, the touch of a teenage boy held no allure. She did all her school work with no prodding from her parents. With all the drug troubles and pregnancies that characterized the lives of their friends' children, Sonia and Max could hardly believe their luck. What they couldn't know until later was that Anna's rebellions were private. She didn't announce it, but she wasn't planning to marry, and at that time in her life, she couldn't imagine ever having children. Her parents couldn't wring their hands over these convictions until years later, when they came up in a practical way. At seventeen, her desire to do well in school and to avoid boys her own age happened to coincide with their own hopes that she would be responsible, studious and chaste.

Anna would never forget one night when she was seventeen. Given her self-imposed nunlike behavior, she was mortified when her father forbade her to sleep at her friend Amy's house after he'd already allowed it. A few hours after granting permission, he learned that an eighteen-year-old boy, a school friend named Stefan, would be staying there, too. Anna assured Max that they would all stay in separate rooms but her father displayed a vehemence of almost emergency proportions, as if it were not only important that she leave that situation but do so as quickly as possible before something disastrously irreversible might occur. Sonia and Max came to pick her up and, feeling openly humiliated and vaguely angry, Anna said good night to Amy and Stefan and went home with her parents.

A few days later the anger began to seep into her consciousness, and she felt betrayed by Max's parental outrage. After behaving with exemplary aplomb all her life, her father went berserk at what turned out to be the first true test of her character. Max watched Anna face the first possibility of making a wrong turn and never for an instant considered trusting her to do the right thing. More than that, the episode destroyed her faith in her father's judgment. He was clearly worrying about all the wrong things.

During Anna's childhood summers she and her family met her parents' Lithuanian and Polish friends at a French spa, Sonia being a devotee of the power of healing waters. Max, no more worshipful of mineral water than of Biblical dictates, would return to New York early August as he always did to prepare for the fall semester, leaving Sonia and Anna on their own for another month.

The days were spent at the beach, where concrete steps met the water's edge in a triumph of French engineering over the sloping silt shoreline of nature. The aerosol cans filled with therapeutic local water glistened from the counters of every *bureau de tabac* as if one couldn't walk to the lake and lap it up for free; the ubiquitous framboise candies that friends brought Sonia by the bushel, *their* mysterious healing powers implied but never articulated, and the sight-seeing tours to Mont Blanc and around Lac Leman, were the odd props of the summer's calm routines. They rose in the mornings for croissants *et* café au lait, walked to the cement *plage* where they rented slatted wooden chairs and tents to change in, bought sweets made of cream and heavily-fatted chocolate for the midafternoon snack, and would dress for dinners served nightly by men in bow ties who spoke enough English to amuse Anna with their accents.

With Max an ocean away, Sonia was the center of male attention at the spa. Anna's mother was beautiful, an extraordinary creature who elicited reactions from strangers that would have been puzzling if Anna weren't so used to them. People in the street were always talking to Sonia. Anna's memory of her mother's beauty was vivid. Perhaps because as her mother aged and her youthful good looks faded, Anna thought of beauty as an inflated commodity. Nothing seemed as beautiful as it once had been. Beauty was once a term Anna had taken seriously. Now, like everything else, the word had become degraded, overused, meaningless. She couldn't use it at all. How often, after all, do you see beauty? Real beauty. Yes, an infrequent rainbow, a magenta sunset now and then. A field of clover could always provoke a sigh of appreciation, but that was nature and Anna was suspicious of the human appreciation of nature. Does a cow standing in a meadow look around and low admiringly at the undulating landscape? If a cow doesn't then surely the human propensity for going on about the sunshine and the flowers is an affectation. That kind of beauty is everywhere, promiscuously strewn about the planet. But a beautiful person, that's rare. A face we might call beautiful is just a collection of physical oddities that separately repel and mesmerize. Beauty is an off-centeredness that produces both serenity and riveting anxiety in the viewer. An overlarge nose in a field of unflawed skin can do it. A crooked brow set over a welcoming alignment of shining eyes could do it, too. Garbo and Elizabeth Taylor? No. Too perfect.

Sonia's face was the work of a master chiseler. In the middle sat a long, angular nose that tipped flirtatiously to the left. It seemed all wrong in the center of that perfect setting and yet it was the cornerstone of her beauty. Her strong jaw and full lower lip formed a base over which intensely brown-black eyes surveyed her realm, for the world really was Sonia's to do with as she pleased. And the young men who fluttered around her seemed not to mind.

Barbara Shulgasser-Parker

THE SUMMER SHE WAS EIGHT, Anna fell in love. The fact that her eight-year-old yearnings had been directed toward the in-convenient person of a thirty-six-year-old man did nothing to deter her ardor. His name was Yves. He lived in Paris and was taking a few days off while waiting for his girlfriend to join him. He taught Anna how to jump into the swimming pool headfirst and swim underwater. He often took her to the hotel coffee bar to ply her with sweet cappuccinos, for which she had recently developed a taste. They spent a great deal of time together. She was happy to note that she was able to make him laugh, although he sometimes laughed when she hadn't said anything funny. Over all, things seemed to be going well, Anna thought, but even at that early age she could detect the fundament of a re-lationship going wrong. In the primordial center of her female self, she knew to expect the worst. She couldn't dispel the nag-ging certainty that Yves's attentions amounted to an artful detour to the affections of Sonia.

Since Anna's bedtime was eight-thirty, sometimes nine in the summer, Yves had time on his hands in the evening. Anna felt anxious about Yves's need for diversion during her absence, and was having trouble falling asleep. He had taken Sonia out several evenings since Max's departure and, Anna noticed, there was a sonorous echo to Sonia's voice that summer that Anna couldn't remember from before. Sonia was speaking in harmonious rather than melodic lines. Her features were clarified, too. Her face seemed more relaxed and also more vivid. She hugged Anna more than usual.

Yves was a blue-eyed racehorse of a man with dark brown curls, a large neck and an athlete's arrogance. He was as physical as Max was cerebral. Anna liked that he played games with her, games that involved running and jumping, games her father never played with her. One night when Sonia had told Anna

118

she was going out for a walk with Yves, Anna was awakened by noises from another room in the hotel suite. She heard Sonia's voice and she heard the baby sitter, Annette, say good night.

Anna realized that she had fallen back to sleep when the voices woke her again.

"You'd better go now," Sonia said.

"But why?" It was Yves.

"I can't do this."

"Why not?"

Anna heard nothing for several seconds.

"I'd like you to leave now," Sonia said again.

"Please."

"Don't raise your voice. You'll wake Anna."

"Well, what are we doing here?"

"You have to leave."

In Anna's drowsy state, she heard footsteps but nothing more. The next morning she vaguely remembered a dream in which Yves was speaking but she couldn't see him. Perhaps he was talking to her from under the water.

THIRTEEN

Sydney rarely visited his old friend Mort Shinsky at the office. Whenever Sydney needed medical care, Mort would come to dispense at the house. Today, however, Sydney sought the professional atmosphere. He wanted the white coat and the antiseptic smell. He hoped to catch Mort in a professional mood. Mort was puzzled but he led Sydney into his office and they each took a chair.

"I know this is crazy," Sydney said, "but just bear with an old man. I want to get married. The woman is a good deal younger, considerably younger."

"Forgive me, but I was under the impression that you were already married. To wife number five, if my arithmetic is correct." Mort, a wiry man who sprouted thick, dark hair from every dermal surface except the top of his head, put his feet on the desk and barked a laugh.

"Let me finish. It's over. Sally moved out. We filed papers."

"Syd, I'm sorry. Condolences, and then congratulations, of course, immediately following."

"It's not really as ridiculous as it seems," Sydney tried to explain. "Sally and I have been having trouble for years. She's just as happy as I am about this."

"As long as everyone is happy."

"Anyway, Anna wants to have children. My children, preferably." Sydney paused, suppressing a smile of pride and sheepishness. He knew he looked like an old fool dazzled by the prospect of youthful and plentiful sex. But he didn't care.

That wasn't completely true. He did care. He was, in fact, a little worried. What happens, not now but some time in the not too distant future, when the blood stops rushing to the groin? That day, whenever it is. Maybe when I'm seventy? Seventy-five? God, seventy-five. I never figured I'd make it *this* far. Will I still be me at seventy-five? Being seventy-five is already grounds for being someone else. Someone with a limp pecker. Limp pecker. Listen to me. I don't talk that way. I don't even think that way. It hasn't even happened to me yet and already I've undergone a personality change. Already I've got some kind of compensatory macho thing going, with the required tough talk to go with it. There probably *would* be a personality change. Me, with a soft organ. I can't imagine it. And with prostate trouble. And pressure urinating. All my friends have that. I've escaped my destiny so far. How, I don't know. My friends talk of nothing else. Brilliant men, original thinkers, professors, their minds troubled by tubes of recalcitrant flesh, issuing daily reports on the urinary tract as hell channel. The pain, the agony, the screaming fire of piss. God. Imagine becoming a childish, leaking victim of the very organ that I've happily allowed to lead me around all my life. It used to point toward pleasure. Now the objects will be pain and humiliation. Suddenly it becomes the enemy, a reminder of what once was and is no longer. Is no longer. That's a good one. Well, I can always make love to her with my tongue. I will always have an appetite to bury my face in her, ingest that sweet aroma that made her laugh when she smelled it on my nose. I will always be able to do that for her. I couldn't live with not being able to make her come. I couldn't live with it. It would change everything. It would change me. In the middle of the night I woke up and smelled the perfume on her neck and looking at her there I wanted to wake her and make love again. But I let her sleep and I sat there thinking about the future. She will have to make her own decisions. I can only tell her what I am willing to do. She can always say no.

"Can this thing be reversed?"

Mort had known Sydney for thirty-five years. "Is that why you're here?" he said. "You could've just called."

"I think I needed to have a formal visit. To get the feel of what I'm doing, right in a gloomy doctor's office. Let the reality of what I'm thinking of doing set in. I have to know if I really think it's reasonable to do this for love. And lust. If I'd called you up we'd have made a tennis date and you'd have said, 'By the way, a vasectomy is reversible but there's no guarantee.' We'd hang up and it wouldn't have really hit me."

"So, is it?"

"What?"

"Reasonable to get cut for love?"

"It feels that way now."

"What if I tell you that we have to put you under, no local anesthetic like the vasectomy. And we can't do it in the office in twenty minutes, either. Reversals are more complicated. We're sewing together two little tubes about as thick as angel-hair spaghetti strands. So, of course, you'd be in a hospital. Frankly, I'd be worried about your age. You're in good enough shape, but you put someone under and you never know what's going to happen. Even to a child. With general, the dangers start multiplying. Mortal dangers. Never mind the possibility of infection at the site of the wound—the incisions are bigger than before. In any case, you'll be goddamned sore and swollen for a week. And then there's the outcome. After all the discomfort and danger, there's still only a fifty-fifty chance it'll work." Mort was examining his hairy fingers as he spoke. "Maybe less, since you had yours, what, fifteen years ago? I think reason dictates that if your looming marriage is dependent on your being able to procreate, you may go through this ordeal, find you're still shooting blanks, and lose the woman anyway."

"Yes, I've considered that. But at least I will have gone down fighting."

Mort hit his desk blotter with a drug-sample container shaped like an arrow. "You're a stupid old fart, Syd."

Sydney laughed. "I know. Set something up for me with the urologist, will you? Just for a consult. Or do I have to do it?"

"I'll do it. I don't approve, but I'll do it."

"You don't have to approve. Just wish me luck."

"Good luck," he said. As he walked out the door, Sydney smiled. He wished he could go home and start making babies now.

GETTING CUT
FOR LOVE

FOURTEEN

She thinks I'm out of her life this easy? Gregory was sitting by the telephone in his brother's spare room. He intended to call Anna but his fingers were too heavy to lift. He imagined lifting them. Yes, it would be gratifying to press the buttons on the telephone, ring up that familiar number, hear Anna punch out her distracted "hello," her voice protesting the intrusion. But then she'd hear it was him. She would invite him to the apartment. He knew she would. "She misses me," he said aloud. The sound of his voice startled him.

Fumbling, he managed to dial the number. "Hello, Anna?" He plunged ahead. "I love you," he coughed. He issued this announcement like a media alert, an urgent bulletin. News. She'll *have* to take me back, he thought. "I can't live without you," he went on, rasping. "Nothing has meaning without you." His voice was a rumble, a seismic foretelling on the emotional landscape. "You were a fool to leave me," the rumble continued. "I might as well kill myself. There is no life without you. Do you see that? You have to come to your senses and come back. Who will read your work? You'll atrophy without me."

Horrified, but also rapt by the performance, Anna recognized the voice all too well. And the technique. Another of Gregory's overdramatic manipulations, a profession not just of love, plain old love, but of exorbitant love. The extraordinary Gregory announcing his awe-inspiring love.

"I'll *atrophy*?" Here he is, lolling in self-pity and megalomania, and he predicts *my* paralysis? she thought. "Gregory, Gregory, stop. You can't do this." The words exploded out of her mouth. There was no point in attempting kindness. "Who gave you permission? You're raving. I don't have to listen anymore. You call me up, passionate and self-righteous. It doesn't make me love you. It annoys me. And, God, you're *drunk*. You'd never have the courage to call me sober. You're not going to win my affection by reminding me of exactly why I left you."

She hung up, infuriated, the wounds reopened.

Gregory held the phone to his ear with the dial tone a loud, angry pulse against his temple. I have to make her remember how much she loves me. I can't live this way. I want to die. He dropped the receiver and began to weep, wiping his eyes on his sleeve. I want to die. I can't stand this pain. *Then* she'll miss me. If I'm dead. Then she'll want me and it will be too late. Let her have *that* on her conscience.

ANNA INSPECTED HERSELF in the mirror. That serene brow was disturbed, a sharp dent of protest and frustration forming over her left eye. She had been contemplating Gregory's threatening words for an hour. I have no time for this, she thought with irritation. She was on her way to meet Sydney for dinner, no picnic either. A big decision. She was planning to say yes to him, to marriage. Why not? She had said yes and then no so many times in the last week it was now hard to remember where she and Sydney were or how they had gotten there.

SOMEHOW, REELING ALONG the Evanston sidewalk, Gregory settled himself into a Chicago-bound cab. Slumped in his seat, he
nervously fingered a vial of Seconals. Captain Queeg in a taxi-
cab, plotting his paltry revenge. Gregory surmised that Anna
would not experience the full impact of his suicide if he were
to kill himself at his brother's. Guilt dilutes by the mile.

He was already drunk. Maintenance was the thing now. His
plan was to tank up with gin at the house, continue from a flask
in the cab, then gulp the pills halfway to the apartment. Timing,
he thought smugly. Everything is timing.

ANNA DRESSED SLOWLY. As she was about to leave the house,
the doorman called to say she had a guest. "Mr. Gresham," he
announced. "Christ!" she cried. For one calculating moment she
looked toward the fire escape. Twenty-six flights of iron steps in
high heels? Well, I can't leave him down there. He'll tear the
lobby apart if I don't let him up, and I'll run into him in the
lobby if I try to leave without talking to him. "Send him up,"
she told the doorman.

Minutes later, Gregory stumbled through Anna's door. Nearly
incoherent, he shouted, "I adore you." Then he lunged, grabbed
at her, and kissed her. She tried to push him away but he held
fast and she, knowing his strength and vehemence, didn't struggle long, only thinking she could never have imagined herself,
so sane and sensible, brawling with anyone, let alone Gregory.
Yet here she was, knocking down chairs as she tried to wriggle
out of his arms. Gregory seemed to be all around her and for a
moment a titillating memory was spurred and Anna began to
enjoy the kiss; then, regaining her composure, she leveraged her
way out and, in a thoughtful gesture, slapped him hard.

Gregory reached for her again and tried to lead her to the
couch. She resisted. "I'm on my way out. I have to go. I want

you to leave." She tried not to raise her voice but fear drove the volume up.

"Let's just talk," he said, still pulling on her. "I've missed you so. I need to talk to you." He moved her to the couch, holding her hand, stroking it. Then he looked at her. His eyes, a ceramic, shining blue and slightly turned up at the outside corners, seemed to have lost their violence.

"Right after we first met," he said, "when I knew you were coming to the performance, I was so nervous, so excited." He was speaking quietly. "I remember being in the middle of something onstage, speaking my lines and wondering if you were there. I thought, 'This is for Schopenhauer. Let 'er rip.' And after, when the review came out and I thought your sentiments were sincere, I thought, Well, all right. The play's good."

Don't let him take you in with this saccharin reminiscence, she warned herself. "I was the litmus?"

"Yeah. I knew it was all right then." They looked at each other for a long moment.

"Look, I know I'm half-crocked and not in possession of my faculties, if I ever have been where you were concerned. Please, let's get married."

Again marriage! she thought.

"I'll do anything. I'll convert."

He had broken the reverie. Drunk, he was audacious enough to say the right things, the romantic things, but also out of control enough to go too far, to revert to his cartoonish exaggerations.

"You'll what?"

"I'll become Jewish. I didn't want to before. I always thought: Who will save the Jews? The world needs the good Christian. It does. But under the circumstances I'm willing to make the sacrifice."

Anna began to laugh. "Gregory, this is a joke. You're out of your mind. Where did you get this? That's never been the issue with us. I can't believe I'm having this discussion with you. You're smashed. You don't know what you're saying. You won't remember it tomorrow. You can't make promises in this condition. You bust in here shouting about love as if no one had ever loved before. The fact is you're not here for me, out of love for me. You're just here to execute another coup. You shout about your love for me like someone delivering a message in skywriting. It's not aimed at a specific object of affection. You just want to make public demonstration of the vastness of your emotional reserves—your boundlessness as a lover. All of which leads inevitably to proof of your boundlessness as a great artist. Great artists, you think, love hard and drink hard. Please, enough of this. I don't feel like the object of your affection. I just feel like some convenient warm body over which you can pour your syrupy endearments. You aim your love at me and I am expected to drop my weapon and surrender. I don't know why I'm bothering to protest. You're too drunk to even take offense. But I can't help it. I'm furious. I realize that right at this moment I desperately want to offend you. I want to hurt you. Maybe then you'll go away. You have no right." Tears streamed down her face.

Gregory looked at her sleepily but his voice was still strong. "You're right," he said. "I can't tell you any of this now. You won't believe me. I see it in your eyes. I see that you may never believe me again." His eyes seemed to have sunken deeper into their sockets. "I'm just a victim. I'm a Jew in a Nazi world. The verdict is in on me, isn't it? Nothing I say will change it. No forgiveness for me. You're absolutely right. It's the same story as the Nuremberg trials. Never should've had them. Just should've fried those Nazi bastards. They would've done it to us if they'd won. They would've butchered us if it'd been the other way around." His voice was growing less distinct. His lips were going blubbery around the words. "You're right. I've been a pig. I don't deserve justice. Just shoot me. Put me out of my misery." He was slurring his words now and his eyelids were fluttering. "I have so much to tell you, but not now. Later. Wait until later. Later."

He closed his eyes and Anna thought he was about to weep. Then she saw the muscles of his face lose their tension. He slumped on the sofa. "Gregory?" She shook him. "Gregory. Wake up. Get up. You have to go." He didn't move. "What's wrong?" She shook him again, looking at the ceiling as if someone reasonable up there could rectify this mess for her. Now she had a passed-out drunk in her living room and a jealous lover waiting with dinner. Get him in a cab, she thought. Take him to a hotel. Just get him out. Anna shook Gregory again but he was unresponsive. She shook him harder, pinched his cheeks. Nothing. A feeling of panic entered her system. "Gregory, what have you done?" She tried to lift him from the couch and he opened his eyes. "Have you taken something? Pills? Gregory, what have you taken?" She was yelling now, trying to haul him to his feet. "I don't want to live without you," he managed to say.

"Oh, Gregory, this is so ridiculous." She ran to the telephone and dialed 911. "You can't have committed suicide. It's so corny."

WHEN THE AMBULANCE arrived, Anna moved to follow Gregory into the back of the van but the attendant blocked her. "I'm the wife," she said with no enthusiasm as she pushed past him. Riding with Gregory, who was immediately hooked up to fluids and oxygen, she willed herself to feel relief, to suspend her disbelief in the ability of the medical system to redress ills. She allowed herself to think that just because he was now out of her hands and in the hands of professionals that he would be all right, that he wouldn't die. When they strapped him into the gurney, it was as good as telling her he would make it.

But once in the hospital, seeing the speed and seriousness with which his condition was addressed, her fear returned. "Is he going to be all right?" she asked a man in white rushing to Gregory's stall.

"Just wait over there. We'll let you know."

She telephoned Sydney that dinner was off. "They're working on him in the emergency room now. I'm calling his daughter. See if someone can come. God, I don't even know if they can move him. If he has to stay overnight."

"Do you want me to come?" Sydney asked.

"There's no reason for you to get involved," she said. "I'm not trying to keep you away, but it's a mess and, assuming he lives, he and I will have something to straighten out."

"All right." Sydney sounded drained.

"I know you want to help and that you also worry about Gregory and me. Don't worry. It's over. There is nothing to be jealous of," she told him. Her exasperation over Gregory was coming through. "I'll call you later. I'm sorry I sound this way."

HOURS LATER, AN orderly moved Gregory to a semiprivate room for, as the doctor put it, observation. Anna stayed with him. Despite his bulk, Gregory seemed small and fragile under the bedclothes, shrunken by the ordeal. His gown was hiked at the sleeve so the nurses could check the IVs. His arms, gray and large, lay on either side of a tubular midsection, stirring only to the rhythm of his breath. His nose, usually grand, like some bent prehensile appendage, protruded more than usual. Yet even stricken, he looked imperious, De Gaulle-ish. His sparse hair was smoothed; someone had brushed it.

TEARS FORMED IN Anna's eyes as she watched him breathe. Why am I crying? Stop sentimentalizing, she countermanded.

THE NIGHT PASSED. Gregory opened his eyes. He saw Anna and weakly said, "Hi."

"Feeling better?" She was holding his hand. He nodded. They sat in silence for some time. The light was brightening through the window as the sun rose, and it cast a golden outline around his face and hair.

"What did I do?" Gregory asked meekly. Anna explained. Gregory winced.

"Thank you for being here," he said. "I am an idiot. But I do love you. I guess this proves that."

"Don't get me angry again, Gregory. You know as well as I do that I have nothing to do with this. This is just you. You're not some vapid shell who can't endure without the woman who left you. All the love in the world couldn't have made you do this. You just woke up one day and found you'd lost your enthusiasm for what happens next. I'm sure it's temporary. You momentarily drew a blank. You don't want to die. Although you probably did want to scare me. But you don't want to die. You can't pin this rap on me. And that's what you're trying to do. You could've stayed in Evanston. You like having someone to blame. But I'm not taking the blame."

Gregory rubbed his eyes. As his vision cleared and consciousness fully returned, he found himself distressingly sober and therefore responsible for holding a conversation, a dialogue, a debate he might lose. Now he was frightened. God, I could use a drink, he thought.

"Please, okay, I need your help. I'll go to AA, get rehab, see a shrink if you want me to, if you think that would help. I'll fix myself. I'll do whatever you want me to, whatever it will take."

What am I blubbering? I can hardly *think* sober. How can I be expected to carry on my life?

"A shrink? You? See a shrink?" Anna laughed bitterly. "You, the debunker of psychiatric therapy? You don't go to a shrink because someone else wants you to unless you've made a deal with a prosecutor. This is part of your problem. You think you can bargain your way out of everything. Prepare to make the great sacrifice of doing something you believe is ridiculous just to demonstrate your commitment. All that it demonstrates is that you think you can put one over on everyone. Again. Another triumph of Gregory over the lesser mortals who populate his life. Just how much smarter than the rest of us do you think you are? Yes, sure, you would see a shrink, and when it didn't work in the first three minutes you'd bellow about what a racket psychiatry is and blame me for having made you go. No thank you. And what am I even talking about? We're not getting back together. Gregory, God, you're good. You've got me speaking in the conditional, in the future tense. We have no future. Not even grammatically." She put her hands in her lap and sighed.

I MUST CALL Sydney, Anna thought as she walked into the morning chill. Light gray clouds were churning over the dark gray lake. She turned quickly. A man who looked, she thought, like Gregory passed. No, she realized on closer examination, not even close. It was his broken-in jeans and worn-down sneakers that fooled her. What is this man doing, this man in his forties, dressed like a kid in a playground? There are no more grown-ups, she thought. Once you could recognize a grown-up. An adult male had on a tie and jacket, and a hat with a wide brim. She was angry now. A real grown-up had a shadow of seriousness cast over the bridge of his nose. Used to be kids couldn't wait to grow up and dress like that. Now it's the other way around. Now, grown-ups dress like kids, whip off their suits and ties the minute they get home from work. Baby boomers, who brought their jeans with them into adulthood, changed everything, ruined everything. Now you can't tell who's who. Now wrinkled faces, drooping posteriors, expanding scrota, sagging breasts and wattled jaws, they're all encased in denim and sneakers. People impersonating memories of their younger selves.

Anna could smell Lake Michigan a few blocks away, the odor riding on a gust of air outside the hospital door. She turned, hunched her shoulders and walked into the wind.

FIFTEEN

Sonia was in the kitchen making preparations. Max, who had been searching the house for her, entered. He was wearing a faded old shirt and chinos with dark stains at the knees.

"There you are," he said. "Did you order the whitefish?"

"Ten pounds."

"That will be enough? How many are coming?"

"Fifty, I think. Who can tell? People have a tendency to show up unannounced. It will be enough. I have herring, the beet salad, whitefish, stroganoff, stuffed cabbage, tongue with sour sauce and mushrooms and onions in sour cream."

"No potatoes?" Max was alarmed.

"Potatoes, of course potatoes. Or should I have kugel?"

"What kind of question is that? A meal is not complete without potatoes. It's a whaddayacallit, a member food, a food group. Very important to proper health."

"There's going to be plenty of food. You'll be eating groups for a week."

Sonia noticed a bandage on Max's right hand.

"What happened to you?"

"I burned myself."

"How did you burn yourself?"

"I was working on the plumbing." He pronounced it *plumbing*, as if he felt every consonant deserved proper enunciation and those who omitted the "b" were in impolite defiance of the rules of English.

Sonia was more guarded about her consonants and viewed it a reprieve when there was one the consensus allowed her to drop.

"What plumbing?"

"The faucet in the basement."

"That's where you disappeared this afternoon. You *burned* yourself?"

Max shrugged.

"You're a menace. I've never heard of someone burning himself fixing the plumbing. No more fiddling with the electricity. You're likely to drown."

"For electrical work I wear a life preserver."

Sonia was making lists at her desk. Her copy of *The Atlantic* was nearby, and she pushed it under some papers.

"Are you all right?" Max asked.

"Do you love me?"

"Do I love you? Do I love you? Are you kidding?"

During the flight from Chicago to New York Anna had hoped to do some work, and her notebook was out. But her head was bursting with the numerous troubles that required her deep and considered thought—breaking off with Gregory, starting up with Sydney, her parents' reaction to the story, the possibility of hearing from that swine Misha. She scarcely had enough time to list the issues, never mind come to any conclusions about them. What would her mother, who had nearly married Misha, say about the story? Anna could imagine that conversation. "How could you do it?" her mother might say accusingly. Those two parallel vertical lines above the bridge of my mother's nose will be cutting into her forehead over this one. There might be a raising of voices, tears. Or maybe she'll put her arms around me and say she's sorry I had to go through such a thing with someone who was, after all, a friend of hers. Tears, oh yes. But, in the end, she and her mother loved each other, and all would subside, Anna was sure, and a sense of comprehension and settlement would finalize the discussion. They would have a good cry together and feel better about everything.

Her father's reticence on emotional matters would make it impossible for her to fathom his reaction. A good guess was a lot of philosophizing and rationalizations. "It's all in the past. As long as you're all right. Let bygones be bygones. Find forgiveness in your heart. We'll all find forgiveness."

Then again, he might throw equanimity overboard and threaten to kill the bastard if they ever met again. Perhaps her father was possessed of a violent temper that had always been held in check but awaiting the one intolerable outrage. Perhaps he would be angry with *her* for writing about such personal stuff, stuff that could reflect badly on the family. Who could tell?

She jotted some of these notions on a large yellow legal pad. Oh, god. What if Misha actually shows up at the party? she thought. Her faced flushed with hectic red spots and she could feel perspiration push up through the pores in the back of her neck. What if?

ANNA ENTERED THE dining room of her parents' house carrying a platter for the buffet table. Misha, who looked as young and sleek as he did the first time he kissed her twenty years before, entered. He walked straight up to Anna and kissed her hello. She slapped him hard.

Barbara Shulgasser-Parker

"What was that for?"
"What you did was unforgivable."

No, Anna reconsidered. Too dramatic. Silly. I'd probably knock him over. He's *old*. What about this?

Misha had come, too, all the way from Boston. As usual, he was there without his wife, Angel, an American. Among the Litvaks this was more than a simple national label. "American" also meant over-protected, lucky, spoiled. It often meant dull. Anna grew up surrounded by Eastern European Jews and when the rare American adult—even a Jewish one, like Angel—infiltrated her parents' circle, the difference be-tween American ways and Litvak ways were too striking to ignore. Anna was surprised to learn when she was about ten years old that it was possible to be American and Jewish, too. There were a few Americans in the group but they had all, Anna could see, taken pains to accom-modate this other way of living. Angel had not adapted like some of the American spouses had to the oddities of the Lithuanians. Among such a collection of loons Angel stood out as particularly humorless and literal-minded. This might be perfectly normal in ordinary company, but here, cast out in a sea of crazy people—laughers, singers, re-creators of the past—she seemed the maladjusted one. No one was surprised that Misha often left Angel home to deepen her preternatural suntan at their Palm Beach winter place. Everyone would politely ask after her, pre-tending to care how she was while he pretended to know. "Fine. She sends her regards," he would say. Anna expected that tonight, as always, Misha would drink enough to loosen him from his fastidiousness. He would remove his hand-stitched jacket and undo his tie. He would shed what little inhibition girded him with a heavy breath, like someone stepping out of tight underwear. He would probably stop to dance with his favorite women and maybe flirt meaninglessly with Anna, as he had been doing since she was thirteen. She used to think he was making fun of her. Now, twenty years later, she could see that the mock sexuality was the only way he knew how to communicate with her. Then he would head for the piano and sing Russian love songs. The group would respond by keeping his drinks fresh and singing along, weeping.

Max didn't sing. His friendship with Misha was cordial, but serving food and drink to this frequent guest always seemed a moral chore, a campaign launched to prevent a breach of security. Society needed to be protected from this man, and Max seemed to believe that he alone understood this and was capable of doing anything about it. So Max would always stay up until four in the morning, if necessary, reminiscing, eating, drinking. He would even laugh, but it was no fun. It was more like guard duty. Who knows what virgins Misha might be defiling if not for Max's vigilance. Maybe Anna, god forbid. But she was too sensible for that.

WHAT THE HELL am I doing? Anna set down her pen and listened to the hum of the jet engines filling the coach section.

SHE HAD A platter of whitefish on one arm and was heading from the kitchen to the dining room. Standing there in the front hallway, he was smiling, looking splendid and pleased to see her. They were alone and she felt cornered.

"I tried to tell you when I called." Misha's hand somehow alighted on her shoulder without her seeing how it had got there.

"You look wonderful." He moved toward her for a closer look. She stepped back, dramatically enough to let him read her coldness.

"Don't push me," she said quietly. "The older I get the less patience I have for bullshit."

"What boolsheet? Where is the boolsheet? I said you look wonderful. Is that a crime?"

Anna immediately thought of Arletty, the French actress tarred as a collaborator after she rather conveniently took up with a German officer during the occupation of Paris. When Paris was liberated she was arrested and sentenced to death. For some reason, after three months, she was released without trial. Years later she would remark, "Nobody in-formed me that love was a crime." Of course, she was a self-described anarchist.

Anna was ready to attack but stopped herself. He is an insect, she told herself. Less than an animal. He doesn't merit my anger.

"Look," she spat, "let's just carry on as polite acquaintances so that we can both be in the same room together without embarrassing my parents and ruining their party."

"What is it I have done? Do you want me to apologize for some-thing? Did I do something to you? Tell me how I offended you." He reached for her hand. She whipped it away.

"I don't have to tell you what you are. It's bad enough for you that you have to live with yourself. Why make it a topic for conversation?"

"Why are you doing this? I came here to see you."

"Then you made a big mistake."

"Why can't we be friends?"

Exasperated, and feeling the weight of the tray, she gave up the lecture.

"Oh god, okay, we are friends. Great friends, all right? Just leave me alone."

"That's not friendship."

"I would consider your leaving me alone, for the rest of my life, an act of friendship. And speaking of friends, I'll bet my mother and father will be thrilled to see you." Anna moved back toward the kitchen. Finally feeling her back against the door, she shoved it open and left Misha. Once in the kitchen, she realized that she was still carrying the whitefish.

MAX PICKED ANNA up at the airport. The drive home was full of newsy chitchat and she felt that overall her father would not be an antagonist, and that was a relief. Her first steps into the house always sent her into a time trip to the past. The vestibule of her childhood. Here were the flagstone tiles on which she roller-skated against her mother's orders. There was the crack in the marble end table that resulted when she dropped an entire earthenware bowl full of shrimp onto it and the carpet below. The cocktail sauce had spilled everywhere. Miraculously no stain remained.

"Today," Sonia was always telling Anna, "I wouldn't change houses for anything. I did come close to swinging from the trees at first—thirty years ago there was hardly a place to buy a loaf of bread within ten miles. But I began to see how nice a little solitude could be. And getting into the city was not such a big production. Your father was right. About *this*."

When Anna was a little girl, Sonia used to take the child into Manhattan for the day. They would eat lunch together. They would walk. Anna could talk to her mother and know she would be understood. From the time she was twelve, Anna had attended private schools in Manhattan, taking the train in early every morning alone. So the trip itself was nothing special. The real treat was spending the day with her mother, whom she adored. People stared at Sonia in the street. Her black straight hair, uncompromising posture and cleanly architectural features were a rebuke to the less good-looking. She was so clearly a superior creature, lavished with the luck of the well made, that the only natural response to her appearance and bearing was awe. Yet there was something disarming about her—a sophistication combined with girlishness that invited sympathy and affection. Strangers liked her, and each of Sonia's friends considered her a *best* friend. She gave a smile easily, and people dropped all defenses around her.

Hurrying New Yorkers let Sonia onto escalators first, ushered her into revolving doors, gave her their cabs. Shopkeepers kept her in their stores with small talk just to have her around. Anna wished she had her mother's exotic look and manner. "Where do you come from?" people would ask Sonia, wondering about the accent but implying a deeper curiosity, a suspicion that she was perhaps from another realm, another world. As a girl, Anna already knew that she would never possess her mother's other worldly qualities. But now that Anna was grown, Sonia, as much as she cherished her daughter, was perhaps, just a little, the envious one. Anna was still young and full of possibilities. Sonia knew that her possibilities were limited, as the choices we make in life preclude the choices we didn't make, attractive as they may have been. Marriage, children. Sonia had made those choices and thereby ruled out others. She was fearful that Anna, at thirty-three, might waste her opportunities, mistakenly thinking that they would be available forever, that there was plenty of time. Sonia was undeniably proud that Anna had accomplished much of what Sonia was denied by the war. Anna had a good education, a professional life. Max never wanted Sonia to work and, frankly, she realized today that she had never been strong enough to do it on her own, without his approval, to venture where his support would not follow. She should have kept painting, she lamented now. There would have been a future for her as an illustrator. But she needed the encouragement Max was unwilling or too busy with his own work to provide.

"Stay home. We have money," he told her. "What do you need to knock yourself out?"

SONIA WANTED ANNA to obey, to stay nearby in New York and find a husband, work until children came, then settle down to a cheerful domestic life. At the same time, she knew Anna was only doing what she herself would have done had circumstances been more hospitable. If not for the war, Sonia always thought. Perhaps I am a coward, Sonia wondered, forgetting all that she had done to survive and to save Max and others. "Oh, the war," she would wave off Anna's protests. "Courage is doing something frightening when you have a choice of not doing it. What choice did I have? I was frightened all the time, whether I did something or not. I figured I might as well try to save myself. Nothing I did made me more afraid than I already was. Once a German caught me smuggling. Sure I was scared to smuggle things. I used to walk around with things wrapped around my waist under my clothes—bread to eat and stockings to sell. But I was just as hungry as scared, so I might as well bring in the bread to ghetto. I might as well be scared with a full stomach. So when the guard caught me they took away from me the bread and dragged me out. They used to strap people who did something against the rules to a special pole. To whip them. The guard brought me to an officer and the officer told me to take off my shirt. In front of everyone. I thought, 'This is it. What difference does it make?' I looked at this officer and I said, 'No. You just want to look at me, to look at me with my clothes off. It has nothing to do with what I brought in.' He must have thought I was crazy. He himself looked very sophisticated and civilized. He was probably from a good family. You could see it. His uniform was pressed and he probably had it made for him by a tailor. It fit so well. He had beautiful boots and a moustache that was, you know, very well clipped. I was praying that my indignation would remind him he was behaving barbarically. I don't know why I thought it would have any effect. *Everyone* was behaving barbarically. But he looked like the whole sordid business pricked his conscience and somehow, I don't know why, he left me alone. 'Next time, you'll be shot,' he said and he walked away.

"Courage is really doing what you're afraid of. When you live with fear every minute, you get mixed up. You can't remember what you should be afraid about and what you shouldn't. I wasn't afraid of that officer at that moment. Maybe another I would have been. Maybe if he had been yelling at your father I would have been. All I remember is that I was hungry and tired. It wasn't bravery. The worst that could have happened was that he would shoot me. At that point I wondered whether I would live to see freedom ever again. Now. Later. What's the difference? There is no difference if you die."

But when Sonia reviewed her life in America she felt inconsolably ashamed of what she saw as her failure of nerve. She should have defied Max, just as she defied the guard. She should have become an illustrator. She could have lived with the guilt of leaving Anna home all day. She had lived with much worse. Now Anna was fulfilling her dreams. A career she had, yes, but no life. No marriage. No love. No protector. No children.

ANNA'S RECENT AND ceaseless obsession with thoughts of her parents' death had been exhausting, a fixation so unshakable that she often caught herself envisioning with gory specificity the indignities that age, infirmity and eventual incapacity would force on them. She would occasionally concoct the scenarios of their deaths, stage imaginary variations on the themes, in hospitals or at home. She would be absent or on the scene. She would be a witness or informed by telephone. She would report the event to others or hear it for the first time herself from someone who had been there. The easiest, as she saw it, would be death by accident because it left her bearing the least responsibility, disrupting her life the least with visits, care and incomprehensible medical consultations, on the whole a version minimally jarring to her own uneasy relationship with mortality. Accident had other advantages. It left her remembering her parents in relative good health, with vigor, intelligence and bladder control intact. The alternatives would certainly afford her the opportunity to grimly repay the kindnesses her parents once tendered her. Not that she hadn't ever cared for her parents in difficult times. But seeing parents comfortably through death was not the same as easing their way through the occasional head cold.

She'd been feeling a need to spend time with them, and when Sonia called to say that they were throwing the party for Max, a seventieth birthday party, Anna couldn't say no.

The last time she had been home was for New Year's, Rosh Hashanah, and its holy conclusion ten days later, Yom Kippur. These were the only sincerely celebrated holidays for her father. Anna suspected that for all Max's protestations, somewhere the gravity of his Orthodox upbringing had imprinted an indelible piety on him. He scorned religion, yet he was, in his way, a religious man, a man who loved life and beauty and privately suspected that some power greater than himself had created them and was running things. Once a year, on Rosh Hashanah and Yom Kippur, reverberating with the rituals of his childhood, he wondered if he and his loved ones would be written into the Book of Life for another year.

Gravity was the right word; Anna could see it in his eyes, hear it in his voice. Max rarely cried, and when he did it wasn't a showy business. Tears would pool in his eyes and he would discreetly flick them away when he thought no one was looking. But Anna was always looking. She knew there would be no volcanic nose blowing or mewling or the kind of great sighs that practiced criers give out. He sometimes cried when he was delivering himself of one of his send-off lectures. "Now that you're going away to school . . . ," "Now that you're moving out . . . ," "Now that you've got a new job . . ." But Anna could see that he was growing more sentimental as he aged, and every year for the last decade there was one moment of guaranteed tears from her father. The predictability did nothing to dilute the impact of the phenomenon on Anna. This was still Father Crying, even if she knew it was coming. Every year on the eve of Rosh Hashanah her father would call Anna into the dining room. He would stand before her as he read from the prayer in Hebrew, and then English, a special New Year's blessing fathers say over their children. "May He enable me to meet the obligations of parenthood, to provide amply for your needs, and to guide you toward good and upright character. May He bless all your undertakings, and grant you a long and happy life, together with all the righteous, and the entire household of Israel." And every year her father's eyes would glisten as he spoke the blessing in English. He would close the book, say "Amen," pronouncing it *oh-main,* and kiss Anna. Sometimes she couldn't be sure he was crying until she saw him, with his back turned to her, pull out his handkerchief and dab at his eyes.

Last year she really hadn't wanted to make the trip to New York for the holidays but she joked that she was coming in for her blessing, and when she said it over the telephone to her father she realized that it was no joke. Now she was here, again, for the party. She'd bought him a beautiful new briar pipe. She wished there was more she could have done, but given the events with Gregory and Sydney, she lacked the energy to put more into it.

SONIA HAD NOT said much more about the breakup with Gregory than that she was sorry Anna had to go through it and that it had caused Anna pain. She wanted to say "I told you so," and generally express her glee that Anna was finally free of that drunk. But she held her tongue on the subject. She had other topics to pursue.

"That Sydney Aronson. Isn't he married?" Sonia was speaking

in her Sherlockian register, the flutey, friendly tone she assumed to disguise interrogations, giving away in her first melodic syllables exactly what she sought to hide. The timbre went high, as if innocence were always delivered in coloratura. She would flutter at the top of her range throughout the investigation. Are you two screwing? is what she wanted to know. Now, Anna predicted, Sonia would tell a story about herself and Max, and Anna was to draw a conclusion that would apply to her own ill-advised living arrangements. Max, Sonia now could see, was too old for her, she told Anna as she had many times before, and *they* were only ten years apart. But how could she have known when she was nineteen what ten years' difference would mean to a sixty-year-old? What could she know when Max first swept her off her feet? Nevertheless, Sonia assured her daughter, she adored Max. This was clear. Anna knew they had been through plenty together but now after so many years they had come to see that the match was good, the choice was sound. They belonged with each other. So, for Sonia, there were no regrets. She said.

"Years ago your father was working very hard. The department at Columbia was pressuring him to stay in town more. He was traveling a lot. He was working on two books. He was on television all over the place. It was starting to get hard to remember if I was going to get to see him on any particular night in person or electronically. Then, suddenly, in the middle of all this activity, he wasn't feeling well. His chest is tight. He's calling me from whatever hotel in whatever town, complaining, scaring me. Of course he's not feeling well—he's at the typewriter at six in the morning, he's teaching classes, he's traveling, he's lecturing. How could he feel well?

"Well, first I think: He's ten years older than I. This is to be expected. I was afraid." Sonia drew herself up into the posture for delivering an aside: "This was twenty years ago, I was a young woman. Our life was ahead of us." She sighed. "I kept trying to get him to slow down. To take some time off. To get together with friends, play cards—you know how he loves to play cards. Stop pushing yourself. What's that nursery rhyme? All work and no play makes Jack a dead boy? And *his* father had heart trouble. Your father was always a vigorous man, but this was too much. I wasn't getting anywhere telling him to relax so one night I said to him, finally, and this was so hard to say, 'You're starting to smell like an old man.' Now that's mean, real mean. I couldn't actually keep a straight face. But I had him going for a minute."

"What did he say?" Anna asked.

"Nothing. He laughed, too."

"Did he stop traveling?"

"No, he didn't stop anything. Your father has too much energy. Too much whirling around in his head. Being with your father was always exciting. He is a maverick. He was always fighting authority. He achieved contrary to expectations. He played academic politics even though diplomacy is not his strength. But he did what he had to do, and to all outsiders he seemed to have become the epitome of the academic. It even confused me at first. I would look at him sometimes and wonder, 'Who *is* that?' And it confused him, also, I think. But he needed to do it. He was a foreigner, writing in English, competing with native-borns. The competition was stiff. His department chairman was certain your father was after his job. He must have looked at your father and wondered, 'How can I use this man's talents and yet still contain him?' If I were the chairman, I would have been afraid of Max. It's not just that he was becoming famous, or that he was ruthless and selfish about maintaining his territory and living a life separate from the university, but your father is also a just man. He made a lot of enemies and he was dangerous. You run rings around people long enough and they start shooting at you. People who work with him know he's just and compassionate and loving. He has a secretary who would kill for him. She doesn't let *my* calls through sometimes. But others only saw him as a steamroller of a man.

"I was never the good academic wife. I don't think you can imagine me serving tea to a bunch of ladies. I don't get any pleasure or sense of prestige from your father's position, whatever that is. The status of the wife of a great man is so artificial. And people mostly offered me the hate they held for your father, not the honor.

"So when he started having chest pains, I was beside myself."

Anna was alarmed. "When did he have chest pains?"

"Twenty years ago. You were small. I realized what I never realized before, that I would have been devastated if he had died. I couldn't see myself with anyone else. Who could replace him? He is the most interesting person I know. When he says something, I am genuinely interested. Even if I've heard it before. And at this stage in our lives I have heard most of it before. But that doesn't matter. He is a dear, dear friend.

"Anyway, so I called Grisha to ask him about the chest pains. Grisha isn't a specialist but I thought he could at least advise me. Grisha said not to worry but he also said, 'I don't know who would be worse off if he died, you losing a husband or me my best friend,' and I said, 'Don't be ridiculous. You would still have sex.' "

"You said that to *Grisha*?" Anna was amazed.

"Yeh. Probably not those exact words, but yes. He's a big boy."

"Grisha always seemed so disconnected. Like he'd never heard of sex."

"Oh, he's heard of it." Sonia threw off a knowing look. Anna was startled. Had Sonia slept with Grisha? My mother with Grisha?

"It's not easy to live with someone older," Sonia said. "It's only ten years, but the older you get the more of a difference it makes. I'm sixty. That's a long way from seventy." She paused to cast a significant glance. "This Sydney seems like a very nice man. He's been a good friend to you but what do you suppose he wants with you? Really."

"We're friends. We talk writing."

"I don't doubt that, but there are after all hundreds of people in Chicago with good educations, widely read people, people he could discuss Proust with. I have to think he picked you for other reasons. I mean, in addition to your great mind." She squeezed her mouth into a questioning pout. "I know you've known him for a long time but you just broke up with someone, which of course, was the right thing." She couldn't resist a little jibe. "But it must be lonely. And this Sydney must have some pretty strong feelings for you to remain your friend so long. No? I just don't want to see you do something you'll regret. Sometimes you do things when you're young that seem silly but you're young enough that you can recover from the damage. Just because you're young and there's a lot of time to heal. But you're getting too old to get away with big mistakes. Even with medium mistakes. You made some big ones already."

"Everyone makes mistakes," Anna said. "I haven't done anything that awful."

"You shouldn't be upset. As you say, everyone makes mistakes."

"I shouldn't be upset? Whose mistakes are we talking about?"

"I, uh, I don't know what you mean."

"Oh, Mom."

"What are you talking about?"

"Why bring this up if you clearly don't want to talk about it?"

"I have fifty people coming."

"It's okay. We don't have to talk about it. I thought you wanted to."

"I just said you made some mistakes. We all make mistakes."

"You knew, didn't you?"

Sonia's face looked as if she had been slugged. Welling up in Anna at that moment was the automatic reiteration of the mantra she'd lived by for so long. She believed it would be inappropriate for an adult to be angry about something so much a part of her distant past. At the time of the transgression she could have, with justification, protested, even publicized, her mother's neglect. They could all have worried and fretted over the certainty of a dim future for poor, traumatized Anna. Anna might turn out to be an emotional cripple, everyone could speculate with satisfaction, and there would be good reason for anger and recrimination. But here it was, ten years down the line and, really, how bad was it? While Anna's emotional life was hardly ideal, she didn't fear that she was headed for the psycho ward. She wasn't an emergency case. Except for the fact that her mother had let her down, had failed to protect her, what was really so awful about her life now?

Anna had so long ago decided to take responsibility for the outcome of her life—perhaps in response to the helplessness of the Misha years—that at age thirty-two, she felt being angry at her mother for not stepping in seemed churlish, juvenile.

"You haven't said anything about the story."

Sonia paused before she responded.

"It's a good story. I'm just not sure you had to write it."

"You're ashamed of me."

"Well, it was foolish."

"What was foolish? Writing the story? Or what the story was about?"

"Both."

"I was only a kid. He was a grown-up. I'm not saying I had nothing to do with it, but which of us was acting under the burden of an expectation to behave morally? A thirteen-year-old, or your friend?"

"But you weren't thirteen forever. It went on. You're a smart girl. You knew what you were doing."

"And what was I doing?"

"This was all so long ago. Why do we need to do this?"

"Have you spoken to him about it?"

"No. What would I say?"

"You did know, didn't you?"

Sonia said nothing.

"Why didn't you do something?"

Sonia sighed and the vertical lines above the bridge of her nose deepened. "I thought it would just go away." Sonia said this as if having chosen to deliberately do nothing had been an act of the highest principle. Sonia was defending her entire life as a mother now. It wasn't that she knew she had done the right thing in this matter, but rather that she knew she was a good mother and therefore whatever she did at the time must have been the right thing. "I didn't think it would hurt you. I hoped it wouldn't hurt you. I'm sorry if it did. But I couldn't have stopped him."

Anna reflected on this truth. She knew the issue wasn't whether Misha could have been stopped. It was, in fact, that Sonia could never have been the one to do it. All at once, Anna felt her habitual compassion for Sonia and the self-imposed desire to take responsibility for her own life dematerializing. She bade good-bye to these virtues as they were immediately replaced by a passionate urge to lay blame.

"Yes, you're probably right. *You* couldn't have done anything to stop it." Anna's voice rose a decibel. "Maybe because you were in love with him and didn't want to accept that he could do something so completely—what's a good word for a pervert who also betrays one of his oldest friends all in one act? Heinous? But let me just point out to you that someone else, another person's mother, might have told him to stop or she'd tell his wife, or call the police, or worse yet, never speak to him again. That was the trouble, wasn't it? If you told him off, if you acknowledged what he'd done, you couldn't ever speak to him again. That would have been the end of the affair. You know, maybe that's what I was doing. Just trying to break you two up. Maybe that's how you always saw it and, by god, you weren't going to let a little child molestation get between the two of you." Anna shook her head as she stared at her mother defiantly. "You chose him over me," and at the sound of those painful words, Anna's eyes poured out a torrent that she had held in for years.

In the presence of her daughter weeping, her strong, admired, independent daughter shaking with the pain of childhood abandonment, Sonia, too, began to weep. She reached for Anna. Anna waved her away but Sonia pulled at her daughter violently, and they fell into each other in a desperate clasp.

"I never meant to hurt you," Sonia said between sobs, holding her child to her. "I wasn't in love with him. We were old, old friends. You can't understand what we went through together. He was a damaged person, but basically good. I didn't think he would do anything terrible. I was wrong. You just don't want to believe the worst of someone, even when it's right in front of you." Sonia was rocking Anna in her arms now. "I should have protected you. Please forgive me."

They continued to rock and weep and murmur appeasements

for more than an hour. Beef stroganoff simmered in a large pot in the kitchen. And the evening's guests were showering and dressing in their homes, anticipating another wonderful party at the Schopenhauers'.

SIXTEEN

Every Friday and Saturday of Anna's childhood, her parents either went to another Litvak's house or entertained the crowd, twenty-five or thirty-five at a time, in Scarsdale. From what Anna could tell, each gathering adhered to a winning formula. A great deal of food washed down by a great deal of vodka. Singing, dancing, loud talking, laughter, raised voices, loosened ties, gossiping, drama. The parties had everything, as if each contained in a weekend-night-unit all of life, and these microcosms of life were the antidote to bitter memories of a time when the prospect of the future was by no means assured. And there was sex. When Anna was a child she didn't dwell on episodes she was too young to grasp. But when she was older she would recall scenes she'd witnessed as a child and see them for their blatant carnality. Most of the women dressed carefully to showcase the décolletages enhanced by the good, high-caloric American life, and the men obligingly stared at what was on display. Nine-year-old Anna once saw a drunk Jascha unbuttoning the tight, low-cut sweater of Masha and planting his large hands over her lingerie-festooned bosom.

The residual childishness that spilled onto the parties was understandable. For many of her parents' friends, childhood had been snatched away by Hitler, a man who was known in those circles as the greatest matchmaker in history. What the hell was Boris doing with Ilona? A child of eight could tell they not only didn't belong together but that they openly despised each other. And how did Gita ever consent to a date with Vova, never mind marry him? The greatest matchmaker in history.

When she was a child Anna would already be in bed by the time the parties started. Max and Sonia would creep into Anna's room to show her off to a conga line of tiptoeing friends. Max would hold the door open to let the hall light shine on the child's unconscious form, and, later, after everyone had commented approvingly, he would press the Litvaks to file out quietly, and he would wonder. They were thinking, what? That only a few years ago we would never have imagined spending a Saturday night in a well-heated house free to annoy our spouses, free to admire the loose-lipped pout of a sleeping baby, free for all sorts of pettiness for which people busy being afraid of dying have no time? No. They whispered compliments for the sleeping child but they were not celebrating an ordinary toddler sleeping in peaceful oblivion. It was life itself they were blowing kisses at. This kid could have been born into slavery. Or *never* born. No, it wasn't even that, Max thought. Life simply goes on. The pain stays in the memory bank but only as a vague pinch. The fear. The hunger. Yes, he remembered them. But when he looked at his small daughter, what filled his heart wasn't the fact that no Nazi would steal her from him or snatch youth and innocence from her. No. It was she herself, independent of the triumph that her existence represented, that set him floating in a mist of simultaneous peace and anxiety. She was his. Yes, but his only for another few years. She was already walking and with her first step he felt the anguish of separation, seeing in it her first step away from him, from his love, from his willingness to protect her from what she would one day tell him she did not want to be protected. He saw it all right then. Maybe he saw it before, too. Before she was born. He looked ahead now, not to the gore and terror of his past. Were it all to happen again, would there be anything he could do to save her? No. He knew that all his experience gave him no real edge. It wasn't intention that saved children during the war, or all children would have been saved. He knew of parents who paid to have their children taken across borders and thereby sent those children to death. Thinking they themselves were remaining behind in danger, they survived to live ever after with their guilt. Against irrational horror only luck saves you. Max wasn't better at evading German cruelty than his friends who died. He wasn't smarter. Just luckier. He would watch Sonia tighten the blanket around the child's bump of a shoulder and Max would shudder with love for them both.

"You have a beautiful daughter," Sonia would say to him, and they would close the door and rejoin their guests, leaving it ajar to listen for Anna's bad dreams.

ANNA GREETED FRIENDS of the family she hadn't seen in years. She made drinks. She offered canapés. Many of her parents' friends congratulated her on the publication of her story. She thought she detected a sly wink from a few of her well-wishers, but she cut off conversation before she could be more thoroughly interrogated. Misha hadn't arrived yet. She slipped away upstairs to further postpone their encounter. Sitting in her childhood room she could hear her father's party downstairs. The evening's events had already suggested stories to her. She watched her parents' friends and felt the kinship. I have a Yiddish accent, she thought. A Lithuanian Yiddish accent, like my father has. I don't speak Yiddish, but I grew up in New York, so I might be expected to drone in that nasal New York bleat, that r-dropping, sibilant verbal whine that shapes the New York larynx sometime before puberty. Instead my pronunciation is careful, like a newcomer's, a greenhorn's. Of course, I never had to get rid of a rolling *r* the way my father did when he came here after the war, or struggle over that crazy English *th* sound in all its tongue-defying incarnations—*through, though, this, thing*. I didn't have to make those tricky distinctions between consonants—*loose* and *lose, close* and *close*—or vowels, *wheel* and *will*—that make the difference between one meaning and another. The difference, for example, between the word *sheet* and the word *shit* is practically indiscernible to the oral musculature. Still, the distinction needs to be made. "Boolsheet," my mother says when she wants to be daring, and considering what her palate has to go through to produce that utterance, the exercise is indeed a bold one.

I sound American, I know, but I'm told that when I get upset I lapse into *mitteleuropean*. I pronounce certain tricky words the way I'd first heard them, in childhood, enunciated by the people who taught them to me. These are the words that I later figured out—in adulthood, with embarrassment—I had been misspeaking for years. I still today have to ask myself: *aggravate* or *aaahhgravate*?

European friends of the family used to compliment my parents on their "beautiful English," high praise from people who themselves pronounced it *Hengulsh*. My father learned the new language so well that he made his living in this country as a writer. But Yiddish was spoken in the house. All of my parents' friends spoke Yiddish, and the sound of it always seemed to be everywhere. Loud. Vehement. Someone's face was always red with emotion, someone's neck always studded with engorged blood vessels. Someone was always yelling. Not necessarily in anger. Yelling happens to be the tone of voice most appropriate to Yiddish. The Yiddish mind believes that all communication is a form of strain. A futility in the prospect of ever making someone else understand is at the root of this perceived pressure. Yiddish is the one language in which a single person speaking all by himself can argue. You don't whisper in Yiddish. You *can't* whisper in Yiddish. Yiddish carries.

Jewish history has taught certain unavoidable lessons. For this reason the Yiddishist has a hypersensitivity to annoyance in his vicinity. A Yiddish speaker can not only spot an irritation, but he can recognize the minute distinctions between one category of annoyance and another. *Anyone* can identify a *nudnik*. But how many people in how many languages can distinguish between a *nudnik* and its close but entirely separate relation, a *balgaiva*? No language is better suited to expressing annoyance than Yiddish. The intonation of Yiddish is a song of complaint, of *pre*complaint. Yiddish speakers know that the worst is yet to come, so why not say so? Question marks and accusatory sound effects end every sentence. This is the language in which each verbal declaration rings with, "What kind of fool do you take me for?" Or "Don't think for a minute that you can pull that one on me." The cynicism and expectations of no good come naturally to the language of the diaspora. Only an idiot *wouldn't* expect the worst. Romance, on the other hand, is the opposite. Romance is based on the naïveté of the optimist. Even those who have been burned by love, by necessity, suffer temporary amnesia when that hormonally induced insanity strikes again. Yiddish has no room for such folly. Love beats you up. This is well known. So: Let misfortune befall you once and you're just an unlucky Jew. Twice and there's a word for you. There are *twenty* words for you: *schlemiel, schlemazel, nebbish, na'ar, gneedeh, bulvan, shleppakurah.* In sum, Yiddish is the language of the unpleasant inevitable, of mistreatment, of death. It's the language of the ineluctable bad end.

MAX SURVEYED THE room with pride. Sonia had gone all out for the party. Fifty of his nearest and dearest were schmoozing up and down the tiled foyer, the Persian-carpeted living room and the book-lined den. Max loved the house. How did he ever afford it? How had he come up from under such a ragged past, underfed, abused, a jailbird, a prisoner of war, everything short of concentration camp inmate—not that living in the Kovno ghetto was any picnic. How did he escape from all of that just forty years before to emerge at this unforeseeable point in time at the edge of a new century lacking no luxury? Shaking his head, he lifted the glass of scotch he had just poured for a newly arrived guest, toasted a private salute to his good fortune, took a swig and moved back into the rhythm of the party.

Turning seventy wasn't as difficult as he had imagined it would be. He had been making preparations for old age for some years, telling everyone that he was five years older than he actually was, to which the most frequent response was, "You look wonderful." What does seventy look like? he wondered. How does it feel? He had been hiking his age for so many years that most of his friends were sure he was seventy-five by now. Schoolmates were the best victims, ones he had known sixty years and more, who had all been fiddling with *their* ages in the opposite direction even before he came up with his own little ruse. A momentary seizure of mathematical calculation would come over their faces at the news that Max was so old. "Weren't we in the same *cheder*?" you could see them asking themselves. "How come I'm saying that I'm sixty-two?" Then the puzzlement would clear and with a fact-dislodging shrug—sometimes only noticeable in the way they blinked their eyes—they would reassert their social composure and tell Max how wonderful he looked. No one ever challenged him and, for Max, that took a little of the fun out of the joke.

Forty years ago, when Max was wondering if he would make it out of Kovno alive, he didn't think much about reaching seventy or what pleasures achieving that age might offer. There were obvious enough drawbacks. Walking up stairs was not what it used to be. But, then, he never particularly enjoyed walking up stairs when he had the strength to do it well and heartily. He was in favor of heeding his body's warnings whenever the body spoke up. Getting old was just getting sensible. Eventually you get so sensible it kills you. Which made perfect sense to him. A person with a full set of marbles, painstakingly collected over the years, was doomed to suffer death by sanity overdose. Imagine having the right number of marbles. The instinct would be to always do the proper thing, the sane thing, to speak up at the first sign of injustice, to tell the truth, to be charitable. Exercising such virtue is a time-consuming business. Someone that sensible would be so busy indulging in virtue he wouldn't have time to sit down to a good hot meal. There's too much wrong in the world to right. A person would crumble under the weight of responsibility. Dear Sonia, never much of a collector, was happily low on marbles and would probably last forever. No, she had plenty of marbles, more than Max, he knew. He just liked to tease her. She was looking well, dressed in a beautiful form-fitting jersey gown that emphasized her piquant figure. She had a quality that made you want to have her around. There was almost a desire to take her into one's own system on a permanent basis, ingest her fully. If only one could bite into Sonia, digest her and have her beauty and goodness become a part of you. She swept through the house like Loretta Young, a born hostess whose mission was to put people at ease.

She hadn't, however, gone to much trouble to put Max at ease when they first met. Anything but. He had gone through hell to get her to marry him. In the ghetto he would arrive at her aunt's doorstep—the event carefully timed to coincide with the absence of the aunt—carrying in one coat pocket a bottle of vodka and in the other two glasses. He couldn't bear drinking out of the bottle direct. The vodka was chilled to the temperature of the outdoors where, as a member of the Jewish forced-labor contingent, he cut lumber all day for the Germans, nearly hewing off his thumb one day when he wasn't paying close enough attention. The frigid air, inhospitable to a man, was perfect for vodka. The first few times Sonia sent him away indignantly. He had a reputation. He was a ladies' man, a rascal, a good-time guy. But he wore her down. In the end, Sonia would laugh when he came to visit her. He would have died just to hear her chirpy laughter, to preserve it, to save it from harm, to ensure its being passed on to his children. So he entertained her until she forgot her reservations, lost her resistance to him, forgot he was a ne'er-do-well, a playboy, a bachelor with a past. When a German guard warned her—as she was marching out of the ghetto one morning to shovel snow off the airport runways—that she shouldn't return after work that night, that the ghetto would be liquidated the next day, that the Russians were on their way to chase away the soon-to-be-vanquished Germans, Sonia knew that she would return for Max and try to escape with him.

Sonia was a patient woman, Max thought, and would gracefully wait for people to rearrange their lives to suit her. In some cases, her patience paid off. Anna had come in from Chicago. Max and Sonia could see that she was depressed. But they were relieved. Sonia had actively waited and finally, after five years, Anna had broken it off with Gregory. As much as Sonia and Max disapproved of the man, a Catholic, a divorcé a penniless ruffian as far as they were concerned—though they'd refused to ever meet him to confirm their suppositions—Anna seemed to love him, and her parents quietly acknowledged if not entirely regretted her pain. And her advertising job was still a frustration, they knew. It was better than when she worked at that crazy little alternative newspaper. At least now she was making a living. She said that she was still writing on the side. And there was that magazine story that he still hadn't discussed with her.

▲

Anna enjoyed listening to Max's stories in measured doses, envying with a child's unacknowledged envy a parents' talent. Max's facility with a turn of phrase sometimes seemed a shadow cast over her own literary endeavor. If she weren't his daughter she would certainly have found her father's dainty and mesmerizing technique enthralling, as everyone else seemed to do. It was the overexposure, the inescapability of his tales that could at times turn their telling oppressive. At parties she found him entertaining. She could blend in with the other listeners, who, having heard his stories a little less frequently than she, could love them a little more.

With the other listeners diluting her obligation, Anna could turn away while Max wove his patterns of plot and dialogue. She could even get up at the end of the story just at the point where Max, taking a telltale breath, was about to launch into another tale.

Anna was staring at her father as he spoke. Seventy. He looks good for seventy, she thought. We are a hardy people, nicely formed with details well attended to by our maker. Nice fingernails, good ankles, meaningful chins, fine jaws and, on the whole, excellent wrists, the chiseled knob between hand and forearm an emblem of refinement enduring long after age begins to claim and decay the rest of the body.

Max had managed to keep Rina, a fifty-nine-year-old cousin thrice removed, pinned to her seat through a series of stories and, greased with vodka, he was beginning to move lugubriously through his material once again. She didn't seem to notice, and anyway, a fresh crowd had gathered. Rina, too, was tipsy. A night's worth of apricot sours taken in ladylike sips had magnetized her to the couch. Max, a few vodkas back, interpreted her paralysis as proof of his power to fascinate. He was a bit surprised at Rina's interest and, unaware of her apricot sour consumption, thought she might be making a subtle pass at him. How else could she be sitting through all of this, he wondered. He assumed that his patter, even the downgraded party version, not the lofty academic stuff, was a little over her head. Sonia, taking a break from hostessing, had settled near Max. She sat on the floor, her shoes off, appearing to Max heartachingly young and beautiful, so much so that he nearly lost his place in his story. To him she seemed to be wearing the wonderment of a girl as she listened to a story she'd heard many, many times before.

Sonia was thinking, however, of Misha, whom she saw across the room for the first time. He looked sleek and dangerous, as always. His black hair was shining. His suit was impeccable. He wore a red tie against a miraculously white shirt. Something about the chin held high and the cords in his neck strung tight made everyone turn to watch him. He was built to be admired. The immaculate getup was part of the package. Even in ghetto, his fingernails had always been clean and his clothes pressed. He had worked in the delousing chamber, where lice-ridden soldiers came from the front for scalding showers and changes of clothes. Misha was able to wash, too, at the end of his shift, and he managed to confiscate a "new" pair of trousers, a shirt, a coat, a pair of boots every now and then. He would wait until after the lights were out, after curfew, and bring a pail of steaming water to Sonia and her aunt. Water to wash! No gift could have pleased Sonia more. She used to tell him that she missed more than anything the luxury of a bath and scented soap. Misha told her that the scent of her own skin was perfume enough for him.

"THERE'S NOTHING LIKE a necklace for arthritis," Max was saying. The necklace he referred to was a recent gift he'd given Sonia, who suffered her share of aches and pains.

"Necklaces work especially well with diamonds, and even better when the arthritis is simultaneous with a birthday. Sonia felt better right away." Sonia shook her head and smiled. "I have to write a letter to a medical journal," Max went on. "Of course, it's not the cheapest cure. And it's not covered by Blue Cross. In case of divorce, Sonia gets the children and I get the jewelry." He looked at his wife.

"The stones are so beautiful you don't believe they're genuine. They're good stones. Good size. You can see them with the naked eye." He put his hand on her neck, near the necklace. "This piece here covers birthdays between now and the turn of the century."

"It's beautiful," Rina said.

"You should see it in the sun," Max said. "It shines so. The sun is a funny thing. Everyone makes a big deal over it." He took a sip of his drink. "But it doesn't really serve any useful purpose. It comes out during the day when it's bright. Now, the *moon*, there's a useful thing. Shines when you need it."

AT FIRST MISHA was not going to come to the party. He had decided to turn down the invitation. Not that there was a formal invitation. Whenever he happened to be in New York he attended whatever social event the Litvaks were planning. He was always welcome, he assumed. The flight from Boston took only an hour but Misha fidgeted all the way, twisting in his seat. Anna's story plagued him. What troubled him most was that its prevailing sentiment was somewhere long past anger. Past blaming; it was detachment. Why was he so bothered? Why did he keep going back to it? He had by now read it so many times that this version of events had become more vivid to him than the way it had actually happened. Or was *this* the way it happened? Her version seemed more tidy than the truth, more hard-edged and comprehensible. Not that his recollections contradicted hers. He didn't actually have a recollection. The first time he kissed her; the first time, the second time. A blur. It didn't mean that much, he thought then. I don't really remember. It was probably just a kiss. I couldn't possibly remember what went through my mind then, the way she seems to remember. It was twenty years ago. I was someone else. A different person. Trying to remember why I kissed her—a kiss I don't remember—why I kept calling her, would be like trying to read a stranger's mind. I must've kissed her because I wanted to.

Anna had shaped the unwieldy facts into a unit of coherency. She had pumped the banality of real life with a power that unsettled him; reading her version of ten telescoped years had the impact of an indictment. Perhaps the story only seemed powerful to him. Would anyone else respond so strongly? All he knew was that Anna had reinterpreted ten years of his life as one long, irresponsible indulgence, a premeditated criminal plot to which he had subjected an innocent. Some innocent! he thought. One look at her at the age of eighteen and no one could have mistaken the possessor of that mouth for an innocent. Of course, it is true that probably no one else had kissed it. But that doesn't matter. There had been no plot. Just a series of disconnected spontaneous events. That was the way he saw it. Now that she had catalogued and codified those events in fiction—the story of a crude adult taking liberties with a child—she probably felt better about the whole business. He, on the other hand, faced with the pervasiveness of his influence on her life, felt worse.

Yet there was also something disturbing in knowing that he'd had her in some fundamental way and that she had slipped out of his grasp. All these years, he suddenly realized, he had derived an unconscious comfort in knowing that the last time they had seen each other she wanted *him*, and he had turned her down out of—what was it?—conscience? Who can remember? In the ten years since then, at the parties with her parents, whenever there were reminders of her, he could fondly reminisce, briefly consider calling her to renew the ardor. Out of deference to what he believed were her wishes, he had never called. But he had liked thinking that he could. He enjoyed nurturing the thought that the attraction was enduring, that she thought of him when she was with other men.

So Anna's fiction, the story of a woman who had written off an old passion, was maddening. Her seeming indifference to him in the story and her smug pride in having conquered her obsession dogged him. In her declaration of independence she had stolen something from him. His congregation was now down one worshiper, and the loss made him view himself less of an idol. He was so completely turned inside out by reading the story that he found himself identifying with the *girl*. The girl in the story, he understood, needed consummation. She needed confrontation. She wanted to cleanse her system of the compulsion. Now it was his turn. He wanted that, too. He had to see her.

But coming to the party probably wasn't such a good idea. There was Sonia to deal with, too, and Max. Would he lose them as friends over this? Could he smooth it over? Wouldn't their long friendship count for something? Surely they wouldn't ban him. He would have to apologize to Sonia before she could attack, and slap Max on the back and drink with him. It was risky but he hoped politeness would sail him through the ordeal so that he could have his say with Anna. Angel, who insisted on coming along, could fend for herself.

"How could you invite that shit?" Anna had said to Sonia when she first came home. Sonia looked at her daughter, raised an eyebrow, and said, "I thought you invited him." She and Sydney should get together, Anna thought.

Misha moved to the bar immediately. He needed a calmant before any business could be attended to. Max was mixing drinks. They eyed each other.

"Happy birthday," Misha said as he stuck out his hand. Max didn't take it. Speaking almost directly into Misha's ear, just loudly enough to be heard above the Belafonte record, Max said, "Come into the kitchen. I need another bottle of scotch." Once they were alone, Max continued. "I won't ask you if it's true. I wasn't going to say anything to you. I was going to be civilized. I don't even really know how I feel about all of this. I haven't sorted it out. I've known you for so long. You saved my life once or twice, which as we both know was no big deal since I saved yours right back. But not to say anything about this would just be impossible. Things can just never be the same, no matter how I've felt about you as a friend. This is just too much." Max was looking at the floor, embarrassed for himself at having to discuss such matters and for Misha for what he had done. "I know it was years ago. I know it doesn't seem to matter, I mean there don't seem to be any lasting effects. If I'd never known, it wouldn't matter, I suppose. But I do know. And in my heart it matters.

"I don't want to hit you, not really. Well, maybe a little. Part of me says that throwing you out would be very satisfying but for something that happened twenty years ago, it just doesn't make sense. I suppose the real reason I'm angry at you, after I think of what you did, is that it makes me feel guilty and responsible for the whole thing. Somehow I should have been watching more closely. I could have prevented my daughter's pain. How could I have let it happen? I'm furious at you for making me feel that.

"But did I ever think for a moment that I couldn't leave my daughter in the same room alone with you? Never. I'm having difficulty sorting out how angry I am about what you did to *me*. And that upsets me. I shouldn't be upset for me. I wonder, Have I ever really looked at you? What are you? What does it say about me that I've been your friend? I can't throw you out, but it will never be the same. I thought at first, if I saw you, that I would want to kill you with my hands. But now I look at you and know it would be unnecessary. I look at you and think you're just pathetic. I've seen enough killing. I know what death looks like and you look like a dead man to me." Max took a fifth of scotch with him and left the kitchen.

Misha, whose body had shrunken progressively during Max's speech into the abashed posture of a scolded six-year-old, slumped against a cabinet. He found a handkerchief in an inside pocket and swabbed the moisture from his face. With his right hand, he reached for an open bottle of whisky, but as he raised it to his lips he noticed that he was unable to hold the drink steady. The brown liquid was splashing against the inside of the glass. He wrapped his left hand around the base of the bottle and took a deep slug.

SEVENTEEN

The first moment he could, Misha asked Sonia to dance. He'd be able to talk to her, and mitigate the harshness of the subject by also holding her in his arms.

"No, I don't think so," Sonia said.

"Come on. Dance with me." He reached for her hand and brought her to her feet. She was still resisting.

"I said no."

He reached for her hand again. She swatted him away violently.

He persisted. "Come."

He dragged her off with him as Anna watched. They moved well together, like two old ballet partners who though no longer speaking still lapsed involuntarily into the steps of their more compatible youth. Her father was telling another story to another crowd.

"I don't want to dance," Sonia hissed, trying to wrench herself free. He held her more tightly.

"Neither do I. I have to talk to you. Don't be angry."

"I'm not angry. I'm burning. What kind of game do you

think you've been playing? You're a selfish coward. There aren't enough young things in Boston? You had to pick Anna? Let go of me."

Misha released Sonia and she walked away regally.

As THE PARTY wore on into the early morning hours, Anna and her father found themselves sitting at the kitchen table, a breeze coming in through the open side door, away from the smoke and heat of the crowded living room. The table was covered with dirtied plates, crumpled cocktail napkins, leftover stuffed cabbage and a box of pastries, extra in case the ones on the dessert table ran out. Max was drinking vodka. He had been drinking vodka, mostly, all night. His nose was red. His eyes were wet.

"Anna E. Schopenhauer." Max raised his glass to his daughter. "To Anna E. Schopenhauer. The E is for Emma, which is for Emma Lazarus. But you knew that. In 1946. Did I ever tell you about that time in 1946 in Paris? Yeah, sure I told you. I think I'm about to tell you again. I read an article in the *Reader's Digest*. I was practicing my English. We didn't have a penny so I used to borrow the magazine from the café down the street. The article was about the Statue of Liberty. They talked about the 'Gimmee, gimmee, gimmee' inscription, by Emma Lazarus. As soon as I read it I took the first metro to Avenue Gabriel where the American Embassy was and insisted on seeing the man in charge of visas. I explained to him that I'm just what Emma is looking for."

"Emma couldn't have imagined you if she had tried," Anna said.

"Maybe not. It isn't a very good poem. After all, good poems you don't keep on a statue. You keep it in leather that smells good and looks terrific on a shelf in the library where you don't read it, so it seems even better. That helps a poem's quality a lot. *You* could have imagined me. You would have made me up better than I am." He took a swallow of vodka.

"I'm telling you these stories because you're a story teller. Maybe not as good as I am, but I've had more practice. It's in your blood. You're a writer and you have to write. You have to work hard. You have to watch people. I've seen you do it. I know you're working on something now. I'm very happy about it. I'm sure I don't even have to say to you that you should write about what you know, but sometimes what you know best is something other people don't want anyone else to know. I'm not saying that is a good enough reason to drop it, but just be careful when you write about them. Be kind. Or at least don't be cruel.

That's the least you can do. And not for them, not for their sake. Do it for you. You won't be sorry."

He drained his glass and set it down.

"While I'm telling all the wise things I've learned in seventy years, while I'm in the mood, I want to tell you one more thing. I'm sorry it didn't work out for you and Gregory. But you tried. You tried to love someone, and that's very brave because you can get your heart banged in and sometimes it takes a long time for it to spring back. But you keep trying. It's the only thing that matters. And it's a mitzvah to love. I was lucky. I found your mother and she was the one for me, and I hung on to her for dear life. I know one thing now and I'm more sure of it than anything else. At the end, when you die, the one who has the most love wins."

He poured another finger of vodka and sat the glass directly in front of him. But he didn't drink.

"You know, I had a dream the other night. I knew you were coming for the party. I came home from work and you were waiting for me on the front lawn. I wanted to put you up on my shoulders to play airplane. You didn't ask me to but I sensed you wanted it. And I just couldn't do it. I couldn't lift you. I felt awful."

Anna got up, kissed her father's forehead and returned to the party. She sat on a large, deep sofa, sipped a glass of champagne, and remembered what it was like to look at the world from her father's shoulders. She was disturbed from her reverie by a heavy, radiating heat on the couch next to her. Angel had been dancing and now was descending into the down cushion, picking up a handful of cocktail napkins on the way down. She dabbed her sweat-beaded bosom and blotted the perspiration breaking out through her makeup-caked pores. Exhausting her supply of toweling, she propped her elbows to rise from the low seat, but the perch was unsteady and she flailed unsuccessfully at the napkins on the table. "Grab me some napkins, hon?" she said to Anna. Anna pulled three from the tall pile. "Grab them all," Angel instructed. "Thanks, hon."

After another mopping, she checked her paint job in a compact she had fished out of a bag Anna knew had come in with another woman. She applied her middle finger to her tongue and used the moistened finger to smooth the line of demarcation between the brownish makeup approximating the start of her trompe l'oeil cheekbone hollow, and the reddishness representing what would have been the higher topography of the cheekbone itself, had such a cheekbone existed.

She tamped down her hair, clotted black lariats that the dancing had loosened. The loops and knots that kept the bun at the top of her head had been jostled by a vigorous rumba she had performed in sequined, high-heeled sandals.

"What a party, huh? You haven't even danced," she said to Anna. "Why don't you take a turn around the carpet with Mike?" Mike was what she called Misha.

"No thanks."

"Go ahead. I know he'd love to. He always used to talk about you. He thinks you're very smart."

"Oh?"

He always talks about me? What on earth does he say?

Angel shifted her weight and the sofa adjusted accordingly so that both women were forced to the soft middle in a seemingly conspiratorial huddle.

"I know all about you two," Angel said in a hoarse whisper.

All about? Anna panicked. Misha was cha-cha-ing with Mara. The Belafonte was playing again.

"It's okay," Angel went on. "I mean, I used to be upset about it. He had so many it was hard to keep track. But I thought given your parents and all that he'd know better. It was a little tacky." They sat only inches apart. Anna could feel Angel's dampness. Angel looked into Anna's eyes.

"At first I thought it was pretty harmless, but I got jealous when he started calling you. I heard him a few times when you were at school. And when you came to Boston—yeah, I knew about that—well, I was a loony tune. I don't even want to know what happened. But," she shrugged and smiled, "you were a kid then. And you ain't a kid anymore. The years pass like nothing. I heard about you and your boyfriend breaking up and all. Sorry it didn't work out. But honey, just wait twenty-five years and then it's really downhill. It won't matter if it worked out with him or not. To men, eventually, we're all the same. We're kind of all the same to them in the beginning, too, but not as bad. At least when you're young you have a little advantage. You have some time. They think you're cute. You get them to marry you and then, Christ, let them do whatever they want. They will anyway. The hell with them. I mean, we're not all that different, you and me. You never got married. You're lonely. I'm married and hey, I'm lonely, too. See? We're like sisters." She twisted her torso toward Anna and patted her cheek. "Just have kids. That's my advice. Mike wouldn't let me. He said he was afraid I'd leave him and he'd never see them.

"What a world. Want anything? I'm dying for one of those

chocolate things. Great party. Gotta hand it to your mother. She always throws a great party. Mike always says so."

She hoisted herself, pressing her elbows against the back of the couch. Finally, heaving her weight over her tensing calf muscles, she threw herself upright onto her spike heels and, like a large flan catapulting into space, waddled off toward the pastries.

Anna flew out the French doors into the garden for a bracing immersion in the night air. She could hear the stereo playing inside. Then Misha appeared, dapper and dashing as ever, his hair black and shining like the coat of a panther.

"There you are. I was looking for you."

"Why?"

"To apologize."

"So you think you've done something wrong?"

"Well, did I? You look like you're doing well. You don't look so damaged by my attentions. Aren't you cold?"

Anna was shivering in the night wind. Misha gallantly started to take off his jacket.

"No, thank you."

He continued and threw it around her shoulders. "You're freezing." In the swing of the jacket he managed also to put his arms around her. "Let's dance."

Anna recoiled.

"It's just a dance. You'll warm up."

For a moment Anna allowed him to hold her.

"What was so terrible about what I did? You seemed to like it at the time."

Anna tried to break free but he held fast. "I don't want to have this conversation. It's ridiculous to debate with a child molester."

"But you did like it." Misha set his cheek against Anna's. Then he moved his lips to hers. This seemed to be happening in slow motion to Anna, who simply could not believe the man's gall. As his lips reached hers, she stamped violently on his well-shined oxford, said, "You're unbelievable," and ran into the house, leaving him to limp to a chaise longue.

▲

Anna was in her childhood room, with pen in hand trying to make sense of the night, a night not yet over. To a strict grammarian, how irksome to discover that so little in life conforms to code, how few sequences and episodes terminate properly punctuated. When *is* the end? What encounter signaled an end of the first clause of Misha's life as it intersected with Anna's? She didn't even know. When was the first comma, the first parenthetic clue dictating the direction it would all take? Perhaps he was just the ultimate romantic who wanted to feed the passion by avoiding its execution. Weren't we lovers anyway? What is a lover? In old movies the characters used to refer to the chaste choreography of courtship as "making love," as if they were actually constructing the building blocks of something that would someday, postconsummation, be love. Is it intention that defines a lover? Isn't there a minimal physical-contact requirement?

Where does love go when one party refuses to accept the other party's offer? Anna had a theory based on the preservation of matter accounting for all the fat that dieters lose. It's got to go somewhere, get rearranged, lodged in the atmosphere, congealing every morning over the dewy grass. What about unrequited love? Doesn't it dissolve and float around with Brownian indiscretion, tiny particles knocking into us, undirected and annoying, settling for brief instances like dust into crevices of loneliness with irritating unspecificity, driving the new victims to inexplicably irrational acts? The unrequited love unleashed from the broken-off extramarital fling of a bored housewife might reenter the atmosphere and descend from its origins of suburban ennui as part of the rubric of some single woman's existence. As she breathes the love-contaminated air in her apartment, sediments of yearning fall into her emptiness, stirring up passions for no one in particular. Under this cloud of recycled desire she will then pour passion blindly into the next slob who happens by. This explains a lot of unpromising pairings. If Misha were dead, where would his longings go? Who would they be nipping at now?

Is there such a thing as a recidivist romantic? Arletty notwithstanding, isn't love a crime in the hands of certain irresponsibles? Anna suddenly thought the worst of herself. She had forgiven Misha, but now, ironically, she had become him. Look what she had done to Gregory. And what she was about to do to Sydney. Am I dragging this man down with me for the sake of some evanescent pleasure? Or is he doing that to me?

Sydney will be jealous to hear that Misha showed up. He was right about the story being an invitation. I can be so dumb. Yes, and now, as if it were the natural conclusion to the Misha episode, I must marry Sydney. Follow one mush-brained exertion with another. Marry Sydney. Lay him out on an operating table and cut open his loins, heal him with tender loving care, and screw like crazy. If we get pregnant, then marriage, hooplah. My friends will go crazy. His friends will laugh. What, again? My parents will cry. The press will have a good, thickly headlined joke. The title of his books will be used to describe the marriage. Author of *Younger Women* marries one. A pregnant one. And in ten years I'll be a widow with a ten-year-old. Forty-two, statistically a person as likely to hook up with another man under the age of eighty as to suffer at the hands of a pirate. And if we don't get pregnant? Can I tell him no, after all he's gone through? I love you but you are nonutilitarian? And what if something happens to him on the table? While he's having his plumbing, or "plum-bing," rearranged? What if he comes out a vegetable, or dies? How can I allow him to take this risk? For something that any guy on the street could give me? How did I get to this place? How did I become a ticking biological clock? A statistic? A cliché? One among the many striving postwar babies leading a frustrating life. How, when I spent my life evading clichés, doing what everyone told me I couldn't do, falling for men who were in every way unsuitable? Is that what everyone else was doing, too? It's as if I knew I'd end up with an older man since older men would be the only ones left by the time I figured out I wanted to have a man at all. How is it that after so much bucking of the rules that I should end up exactly in the same boat as millions of other lonesome, childless fools? My life couldn't be more unoriginal. I, certified renegade, am left with only one solution to my difficulties, a solution too absurd and abhorrent to consider. In order to break out of my pattern of idiosyncrasy, I am forced to embrace the normal, the average, the usual.

Sydney says he wants this. How come I'm sure he doesn't, or at least he shouldn't? He'll be grateful to me one day. It will be a kindness to tell him no. He's too honorable. If I let this happen, if I succumb to how I feel about him at this moment and kid myself that the future will take care of itself, then one day he'll see what a mistake it was to marry me, one day when a baby is crying and the diaper perfume is wafting and life is mundane and I'm no longer the blushing girl he somehow thinks I was when he snatched me up. And he'll have suspicious thoughts when he sees me talking to a young man at a party. And I will know exactly when that day has arrived, just as I expected, even if he doesn't yet. I'll see it in his eyes, hear it in an edge in his voice, feel it in the pressure of his hand as he draws me wearily to him.

But how can I give it up? You don't stay human long at the rate I'm going. You have to be connected to something. Unnamed desire, the urge to pair, it's dangerous when it stays unspecified. Desire must be named, targeted. Wanting Sydney is different from wanting *a* Sydney. You have to want *Sydney* every day or you lose yourself. You get hungry every day and that reminds you that you're human, that you have needs. You have to feel that equivalent of hunger in your emotional life. Every day. What is the equivalent? Something like compassion? Empathy for one particular person? The trouble is that compassion and empathy aren't nearly as hearty and resilient and recognizable as hunger, as the acid pulsations of a shrinking belly. That sort of feeling is simple, it's Cro-Magnon, a howling unsilenceable emptiness. That emptiness, if ignored, leads to the whole mechanism's collapse. The urge to love, unfortunately, if it isn't cultivated, will go away long before the body dies. I dug a space in my life for Gregory. But it's closing up. I can see the sand sifting in. It will be so easy to let that space fill itself in with nothingness. Before I know it, the space will be gone and I won't need anyone again.

NOT THE LANGUAGE OF LOVE

EIGHTEEN

James Thurber once wrote, "A woman's place is in the wrong."
So here I am, wrong again. I mean, the world is divided into
couples. I'm not part of a couple, so I'm an aberration, fundamentally wrong. I've kind of given up on men. I'm putting the
effort where I actually think I have a chance at getting things
right, in my work. This novel I'm trying to finish is giving me
sleepless nights, but it's going a lot better than my life. The
advantage of fiction over life is that in life there are no rewrites.
Sydney says that, of course, I'm wrong there, too. He says, for
him, every new wife is a rewrite. I don't know if serial matrimony is a solution for me—I have trouble remembering names.
I just want to finish the damn book. Come up with some un-
forgettable ending, something implausible and tasteless, revolting
and clichéd. I'm hoping to sell it to the movies.

WHEN SHE FIRST glimpsed him at the party, Misha looked older,
smaller and sadder. His paunch was slung over the waistband of
his pants. His hair was a thinned netting of light brown tweed,
only just covering the top of his head. The reflected light
bounced through the sparse old roots, revealing a barren expanse

like a patch of lawn where the seeds weren't taking. Anna thought about turning around and leaving, but their eyes met almost the minute he entered the house. He wanted to walk over to her, to kiss her hello, but recalling their telephone conversation and its abrupt ending, he held back. She had matured well, he thought. She had been a pretty child. Once she had seemed fragile with ghostly white skin and thick black hair cut like a boy's. Now her face held him, the cherry-dark eyes, a mushroom of a nose that was elegantly arched, a spare thin neck that looked almost breakable, and pouted lips with the upper and lower an imperfect fit, their texture like a succulent plum. She seemed formidable and self-possessed. He would have wanted to meet her if he hadn't already known her. They continued to steal glances at each other but she didn't approach him, and he told himself to leave her alone for the moment. Every few minutes he found himself looking for her, watching from across the room as she worked the muscles of her mouth to form the pleasantries of party chatter, her hands flying up to push away a stray lock of hair. He was jealous of the men she spoke to.

After midnight he caught her climbing the stairs and disappearing into the second floor. After five minutes' time, deciding that she was not powdering her nose but avoiding his insistent spying, he went after her.

The Schopenhauers' was a large Scarsdale house arranged on three floors with a maze of confusing hallways. He looked into several rooms on the second floor, then remembered where her childhood room was, a room he had visited before. He knocked and, without waiting, entered. Anna was sitting on her bed holding a pad and pen in her hands. Misha closed the door behind him and took a few steps forward. She put the pen and paper aside. He put his hands in his pockets.

"I'm sorry about the call. I mean, I'm sorry you hung up."

She was looking at him brazenly. He had grown ugly, she

thought. She felt sorry for him. It was one thing to look ordinary all your life and another to lose your looks in the advance toward mortality. One was a state to make peace with; the other a blow at a time of life when blows are not welcome. He looked every minute of seventy. She especially noticed his hands. They were plump and spotted and hummocky where the veins grouped, as if someone had spilled greenish-blue ink over the tops. The nails had grown thick and waxy. His eyes were pouched. His face had become a topographical display of gnarls, protrusions and elevations, the document of a life of emphatic living and high temperament. His face was now, even at rest, condemned to continually and forever report old emotion. His face was a giveaway, a guide to what the careful player could wring out of him. Puzzlement was now an eternal emblem hung across his brow. Contempt would reside the rest of his days about his mouth. Cynicism had widened his nostrils. He sat down beside her.

"What do you want?" he rasped. "Retribution? Apologies? To file suit? What's done is done." Had his teeth always been so yellow? Had he always smelled slightly stale? "I'm sorry if I hurt you," he whispered. "I couldn't stop. I had to *have*. I wanted so badly. Everything. Everyone. I just *wanted*. It's gone away, that feeling. I've been released in a way. When you stop wanting, or only wanting a few particular things, you appreciate more what little you get."

"Then you never wanted me any more than you wanted the rest?"

"No."

"And now?"

"Now very little of interest comes my way. I've stopped expecting."

"What does that leave you with?"

He put the tips of his fingers on her mouth. "With curiosity," he said. "It's a substitute for desire."

"Doesn't that lead to desire? Aren't there other women, aren't you curious about them? Doesn't your curiosity drive you?"

He was staring at her mouth. He moved his hand slowly down her neck, tracing its line. He kissed her and moved back to watch his hand again, now on her breast. She closed her eyes. He kissed the bony spot between her breasts and then withdrew again to look at her.

"Why now?" she asked.

"I am selfish. When you came to see me, it was for you. This time it's for me. Will you do this for me?" His hands were under her pants on her bare hips. She put her hands on his and looked at his hair, at the gray in it, then into his eyes.

"What do you want?" she asked.

"I want to ache for you, but I don't want you to want me," he said.

"Then I won't tell you that I do."

"No. Tell me you don't want me."

She unbuckled his belt.

"I don't. Does that excite you?"

"Yes."

"You're aching, aren't you?"

"Yes."

"You can't have me, you know."

"Yes."

"It's too late." She kissed him as she said yes.

Suddenly, she pulled away and opened her eyes.

"Wait," she said. She looked at him. He was wearing only his shirt and socks and an abandoned expression. He pulled her toward him and kissed her again but she disentangled herself and stood up.

"Wait. I have to put something in." She backed away and then turned to rummage through a dresser drawer. Over her shoulder she said, "Can you please check the door? Sometimes the lock doesn't work."

Misha padded over to the door in his socks and opened it a bit. He felt a sudden wind, but its source didn't alert his suspicion. So when he found himself pounced on from behind and shoved out of Anna's room and into the hallway, when he heard the door slam and click behind him, he didn't at first register what had happened.

Just over the railing, below him, just underneath his bare buttocks, were all his friends and acquaintances of fifty years, singing, drinking vodka, mangling the English language, partying to celebrate the birthday of that excellent fellow, Max, father of the woman who was about to ruin his life.

"Anna, *please*," he whispered, tapping on the locked door. "Please."

On the other side of the door Anna stood in her underwear with her face against the door, not quite smiling, but with her eyes closed. She looked as if she were enjoying those satisfyingly sensual moments just before awaking from a good night's rest.

NINETEEN

Dianne was filing her nails in the bathroom. Anna sat on the toilet, watching.

"I don't understand," said Dianne. "From my experience, men don't want to get married. All the men you know seem to want nothing but marriage. It's as if meeting you saps them of their asshole hormone."

"I keep trying to tell you that they're deranged, and you keep telling me that these days deranged is only a minor drawback considering the alternatives." She looked at her watch. "It's twelve-thirty. I have to go."

SYDNEY WAS SEATED at his favorite restaurant, waiting for Anna. The conversation went better than Anna had hoped. Even if Sydney looked like someone had socked him in the solar plexus, he maintained a veneer of gentlemanly courteousness and aplomb throughout the lunch.

"We'll always be friends," Anna said. "I can't imagine that we wouldn't."

"It isn't my first choice, but of course. Yes."

It wasn't until several months later that Anna began to date again, but with no enthusiasm for the exercise—and that's what it was to her, an exercise. In being human, presumably. She didn't want to lose those muscles.

It was inevitable that one of the interchangeable dates would take her to the overgrown fern place sooner or later. This time, the guy was named Price. She liked looking at Price's mouth as he talked. His lips seemed soft, and speech made them slide against the flat of his front teeth, which charmingly shingled in on themselves. The first time they met she could think of nothing but how nice it might be to kiss him, or at least the man she wished he would turn out to be. At that time, his lips posed the possibility of passion. Yet now, sitting at the table with him, she could see that her wish was not to be fulfilled. Already the lips had lost their magnetism. Price was somewhat more well educated than the others, and he was droning on at a higher level of discourse than most of her dates. The lips began to entice less and more resemble two slugs piled horizontally, or two segmented annelids, wet and red and swollen; something to bisect and see if the ends walked off in opposite directions, as he and Anna would, she admitted to herself, inevitably.

"*Lolita* is a perfect example," he was saying. "Nabokov wrote a paean to a scoundrel and a slut."

"Which one was the scoundrel?" Anna asked.

"Humbert Humbert, of course."

"Not a good name."

"Excuse me?"

"Humbert Humbert is not a good name for a scoundrel. A clown, maybe. An intelligent clown, but not a villain. It's not a scoundrelly name."

Anna heard another voice say, "It's more like a country singer."

She turned to the table next to hers and found Gregory, with, of course, a young woman. A blonde.

"His stage name is Hummy Lee Humbert," Gregory added, smiling.

The mousey woman with him chimed in, too. "I think it does sound like a villain," she opined. "A villain in a sci-fi movie."

"Humbert Humbert? No, dear. There's nobility there. Oh, Kay, this is Anna Schopenhauer. Anna, my wife, Kay."

"How do you do? This is Price."

"Price?" said Gregory, offering his hand over the table. "Nice to meet you."

Rather uncomfortably, Anna leaned away from Gregory's table and resumed the conversation with her date for the rest of what seemed an interminable dinner. But thoughts of Gregory intruded. She had noticed the bottle of Pellegrino on the table. The wife seemed remarkably bland, vacant. But, probably, no more bland or vacant than Price.

When the meal was over, Price jogged down the block to retrieve his car. Anna stood outside the restaurant waiting when she noticed Gregory and Kay several feet away, looking for a cab. Gregory's eye caught hers. He said something to Kay and turned to Anna. By the speed and deliberateness of his approach, she judged that he meant to embrace her when he arrived, and she wasn't sure what she would do then. But he slowed as he drew nearer and only put out his hand. She hesitated, then shook it mechanically. On close inspection she could see that he was sober and looking well.

"Good to see you," Gregory said. They stared at each other for what seemed to Anna a long time. "I have to go," she said, but he reached out and softly touched his fingers to her cheek.

"I have to go," she said again. When she turned to leave she could hear him say, "Take care."

TWENTY

I got the call from New York, and when I arrived the next evening, my father was already in surgery. We stayed in the hospital until three in the morning, waiting for my father to emerge, and for a word with the surgeon. He and two other doctors had removed and replaced the torn-up aorta that was leaking vital fluids into my father's abdomen. The doctor looked exhausted after seven hours of poking around in a bloody chest cavity, and he told us that my father would be sedated for another twenty-four hours. Go home and get some rest, he said. He said it would just upset us to see him postoperatively swollen, with tubes winding in and out of everywhere.

"There's nothing to see now, no one to talk to," the doctor said. "He can't hear you and he can't say anything. There's nothing to see," he said again. He was wrong, of course. My father was still alive then. We could have seen him alive.

Some things stay with you because they are vivid and some things stay with you because they're all you've got. I was not there the moment my father's blood pressure started dropping, the moment the sutures trussing his fraying aorta began to give. I wasn't there as the blood diverted from his circulatory system and started emptying into his thoracic cavity where it could do no good. I was not there when the alarm signaled that his vital signs were failing. I was not there as the ICU team crowded around him like antibodies at the site of an infection. I was not there for the heart massage, the electric shocks, the injections, any of the desperate measures emergency clinicians apply to stem the onslaught of death. I can't remember these events. I can only imagine them. What I can remember is a telephone call, and in that call is the sum of sixty or so minutes of medical frenzy that I didn't witness. I can remember a strange doctor's voice in my ear, solemn words spoken resignedly to me. "We did everything we could." In those words, somewhere, were my father's seventy-one years, his holding me lightly by the thumbs as I fumbled through my first steps, his sliding a worm on the end of my fishing hook, his embracing me after I received a diploma, his holding my fevered forehead, his slipping me a twenty as I headed back to school.

My vocabulary is woefully inadequate. I'm sure if I were able to tell this to you in Yiddish, you would know what I mean.

I realize now that I always thought of my father as unmasculine when he was alive, despite the stories of his ribald past, because he was spindly and unathletic, I suppose. Now, perhaps sanctifying him the way we like to do with the dead, I find myself thinking of him as a large man, at least in spirit and appetite for life. I allow myself to see him as others told me they saw him, as an attractive bon vivant with a European survior's lust for life, silver hair, groomed fingernails, well-cut suits, French-cuffed chemises and many pairs of handmade shoes worn so lightly that they were hardly scuffed on the bottoms. But as I enumerate these attributes, it's as if I'm describing someone else, some charming fellow who isn't my father. I look at photos of him; he has his pipe in his hand, his mouth is open to speak to the photographer or anyone who will listen. He is smiling, thrilled to be alive.

"You shouldn't have, you shouldn't have," he wrote me after I'd sent him a birthday gift. "But as long as you did, let me tell you how much I appreciate it. I really do and it came right in time. The dictator (your mother) had just come out with an edict: No more naked tobacco cans in the house. So I really needed a fancy humidor and it's standing right next to my chair (which is still naked, we await the next edict), and I love it. I am sure it gave you as much pleasure giving it to me as it gave me receiving it. So we are even."

The note I'd sent with the humidor invoked the Jewish blessing that one should live to one hundred and twenty years, the age that ripe old Abraham got to before taking his leave. "And P.S. As for the 120 years," he wrote me, "you just wait and see. I'll make it."

As far as I know, this is one of the few promises my father failed to keep. I'd later learned that he had kept many others that hadn't been made, not aloud anyway. He told me stories all my life. I didn't always know what he was talking about. I had trouble sitting through some of the stories he liked to tell, but I wanted to remember them, believing there was something in them for me that I might be able to assimilate at some later time, perhaps when I was old enough to understand their meaning, perhaps after his death. So I began writing him letters filled with questions about his youth, about the war, about how he started out. I wanted to record his past but I just couldn't absorb it in person. I resisted his storytelling when he targeted me face to face. My concentration would ebb as if in unconscious protest against the force of my father's personality. I wondered how he'd succeeded in the cutthroat world of academics and publishing when he was so uninterested in other forms of competition. I'd never seen him pick up or throw a ball. I'd never seen him try to win at anything other than poker or rummy.

"As for my sportsmanship," he wrote me, "you'd be surprised what a great backhand you need to outsmart your competitors and bring home the pot of lentils every day."

I was also able to communicate on paper that I regarded his accomplishments with some awe, something I could never have told him in person. We both would have been too embarrassed by the sentiment. "My dear child," he replied, "I was always a great admirer of myself and I didn't know why. Now after reading your letter I know. You anointed my head with chicken fat and my cup runneth over. I am glad that you mentioned the 'burden' of supporting a wife and family. Actually, it's not a burden at all. It comes naturally. Human life is a continuous process of giving and taking. This process is so complicated and hard to define that very often you take more than you give by *giving*, and vice versa. In order to maintain one's peace of mind one has to convince oneself that one is neither overgiving nor overtaking. If one thinks that one is giving too much and people are taking advantage, one becomes grouchy, a misanthrope. If one thinks that one takes too much, one loses one's self-esteem and gets depressed. The secret of the good life is in maintaining one's grace and dignity in the giving *and* the taking. That's it."

The thing about death is that no one is immune to the clichés. I, who ordinarily could come up with fifty irritating qualities to describe my father, can remember only what I adored in him. I have a twenty-year-old photograph in which my father and I are sitting in a café with four friends he'd known for forty years each. We are all smiling broadly at the camera. All but my father. He is in profile, staring straight at me, beaming.

I look at this picture today and remember that after my father died, a dear old friend of the family told me that she remembered visiting our new house when I was a small child. "Your father took me to the backyard and started showing me the beginnings of the garden," she told me. "As we walked around, he would say, 'And I planted that one a year ago, and it gives me trouble but I think it will come up nicely if we're patient,' and he'd show me something else and say, 'That one came out of no-where. Look how beautiful it is.' He talked with such pride and all the while you were with us, spinning around like a little top, full of uncontrolled energy and joy, and I had a sense that all his proud gardening talk was really about you."

Last year I really did not want to make the trip to New York for the holidays. But I knew that it would please him, and lately I thought more of pleasing him. I came home, I joked as always, to receive my blessing. That night, while he delivered it, I looked down at the prayer book as he read. "May He enable me to meet the obligations of parenthood, to provide amply for your needs, and to guide you toward good and upright char-acter. . . ." But something was odd, and when I heard his voice waver I peeked up at his face. It was clamped in a wince. Tears dripped down his cheeks. He wept so sorrowfully that his shoul-ders shook and he had to stop until he could compose himself.

In past years I used to think that there was a nostalgic joy in his tears, that the Hebrew words reminded him of his own father blessing him as a boy. Or that he took Yom Kippur as his yearly moment to reminisce over the intermittent rewards fatherhood had brought him. But this time it occurred to me that these were not tears of hope and gladness. I suddenly feared that per-haps these were tears of futility, and my heart seized with shame. He had done all he could, fulfilled all his responsibilities and more. Yet I, godless, unmarried and childless, had not met my end of the bargain. I felt sorry for my father, and for myself because I hadn't pleased him more. I felt my heart knocking in my chest. This was My Father, who hardly ever cried.

"I'm sorry, Dad," I said, but he looked away.

He drove me to the airport a couple of days later. We embraced for a long time. I didn't see him after that.

The only good news here, the only un-Yiddish discovery that I can report, is that death isn't the end of a relationship. For years I've been dreaming about my father at least once a week. Sometimes in the dream I'm aware that he's dead, and I ask him what he's doing there. Other times, the dream's fiction is that he's still alive and everything is as it was. I dreamt the other night that my father came home from work. I was waiting for him on the front lawn. I wanted him to pick me up over his head and play airplane. He rolled up his silk shirtsleeves and said, "My pleasure."

ABOUT THE AUTHOR

BARBARA SHULGASSER-PARKER is a native New Yorker. She attended Sarah Lawrence College, earned a B.A. from City University of New York and an M.S. from the Columbia University Graduate School of Journalism. While a feature writer at the *Waterbury* (CT) *Republican,* she won a NEH grant to study aesthetics at the University of Chicago. She was on staff at the *Chicago Sun-Times* and was a film critic for the *San Francisco Examiner* for thirteen years. She wrote, with Robert Altman, the film *Prêt-à-Porter,* and her work has appeared in *Vanity Fair, The New York Times, Mirabella, Glamour* and the *Chicago Tribune.* She lives in Santa Monica, California, with her husband, Norman Parker.